TROVES OF FANTASY

A COLLECTION OF SHORT STORIES

JOE MEADE

Troves of Fantasy

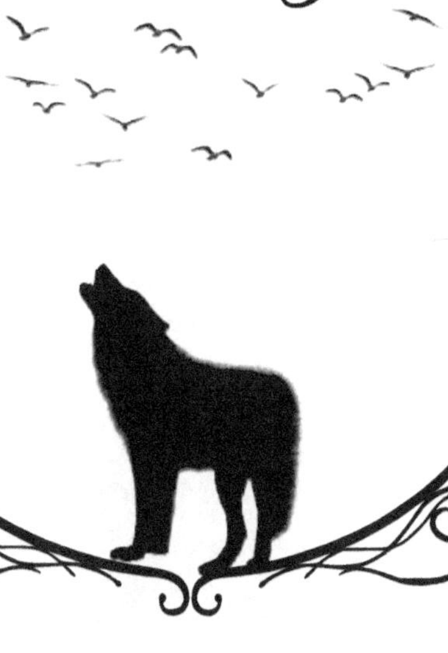

Joe Meade

Copyright © 2018 by Joe Meade.

All rights reserved. No part of this publication may be reproduced, distributed, or transmitted in any form or by any means, including photocopying, recording, or other electronic or mechanical methods, without prior written permission of the publisher, except in the case of brief quotations embodied in critical reviews and certain other noncommercial uses permitted by copyright law. For permission requests, write to the publisher, addressed "Attention: Permissions Coordinator," at the address below.

ARPress

45 Dan Road Suite 36

Canton MA 02021

Hotline: 1(800) 220-7660
Fax: 1(855) 752-6001

Ordering Information:

Quantity Sales. Special discounts are available on quantity purchases by corporations, associations, and others. For details, contact the publisher at the address above.

Printed in the United States of America.

Library of Congress Control Number

ISBN-13   Softcover   979-8-89356-780-9
                 eBook   979-8-89356-779-3

Library of Congress Control Number: 2024942027

Table of Contents

Dedication ....*I*

What Lies Beyond 1

Something's Down There 17

The Shadow's Host 35

A Cry For Help 59

Lady Death 75

The Dreamstone 83

Spirit Warrior 97

The Tormented 143

Cavern Of Hope... 151

A Wolf's cry.. 171

Dedication

First and foremost, I thank the Lord for giving me the will and skill to create and write. I am grateful.

I also want to thank all those who endured listening to and reading my stories, playing the games I created, and entertaining my many ideas long before they came to fruition. Your interest and support, feigned or real, helped me get this far. As a lover of fiction, I choose to believe the latter.

Much thanks!

What Lies Beyond

MUTED THUNDER RUMBLED overhead, and a light mist fell, wetting the red and black cobblestones. I pulled my cloak tighter against a sudden gust of wind. With my head full of troubling thoughts, I turned onto Fate's Way, the aptly named road leading to the Great Door; the reason for the renown of the otherwise unremarkable town of Frozen Cleft.

My shift had ended hours ago, but duty bade my return. Not that I had any intention of going along with Marcus's plan, but the matter had to be dealt with. As a fellow Gateway Guard, Marcus should know better. But he had been anything but rational since his only son, Therris, failed to return from

The Beyond at the last opening of the Great Door, three nights ago.

Admittedly, some of Marcus's accusations held merit. Had anyone lived actually seen anything from *The Beyond?* Had anyone witnessed someone being killed by shadowy demons for speaking of what they saw in there?

I reached inside my cloak and pulled out my medallion by its leather cord. The ivory disc, with its carving of some strange beast glowed a soft white. It would glow for a few days yet before fading back to pale normalcy. Exposing it to the light of a full moon, even for only a few moments would restore its lustrous aura. After drinking in the glow of the moon, it would glow for another two weeks. The curious heirloom was a gift from my father, a well-respected Gateway Guard and former Keeper of the Key.

It disturbed me that my father's life, and now my own, may have been dedicated to a farce. No. Guarding the Great Door and protecting Frozen Cleft from the denizens of *The Beyond* was important. Marcus had to be wrong.

I turned the final corner past a high wall of smooth blocks and paused. The towering cliff face embraced the sacred door like an obsidian mantle. The Great Door, as tall as four men and adorned with cogs, levers, wheels, and handles of polished brass, stood in silent duty.

Where were all the guards? Normally, there would be one Gateway Guard on either side of the door with two more on either side of the road some fifty paces further out. Now, only a solitary figure stood in front of the door; Marcus.

A lantern sat on the ground by Marcus's foot, casting him in devilish shadows. His forest-green cloak flapped loosely about him. He stood casually, with one hand resting on the pommel of his sword.

"Keeper of the Key," Marcus said, giving me the slightest of bows. "I knew you would see reason. Time to expose the lie of the overseer's, *Beyond*." He stressed that last word with clear sarcasm.

"Marcus, I didn't come here to open the Great Door. You know the dangers of opening the door without a full moon. What if you're wrong? What if—"

"What if I'm right?" Marcus said, cutting me off. His tone had taken on a dangerous edge. "My son is in there, Timothy. I want to know what happened to him. I want to know the truth. Overseer Losweng returns tomorrow. I won't waste this chance."

His son had paid the hefty entrance fee to Hectar Losweng, the overseer of Frozen Cleft and owner of the Great Door, and entered *The Beyond* in search of adventure and riches. He, like so many others, never returned.

It wasn't that Overseer Losweng didn't explain that what lay beyond the door was a land of danger and predators as much as it was a land of riches, and it wasn't as if those who entered didn't know that most who chose this path never returned. Just the same, I understood Marcus's pain, but breaching the gateway to *The Beyond* was too great a risk.

The ancient door had not been opened out of the ceremony in over two hundred years. The accounts of that incident say that a swarm of over twenty demons poured forth and killed half the town.

"I can't risk it, Marcus."

"You mindless fool," he said, drawing his sword.

Marcus's sword had barely cleared its scabbard before I had my own sword drawn and held to his throat. "Let this go, Marcus. I don't want to hurt you."

He stared back with wild eyes. His long, brown hair hung down in a wet mess over much of his face. He smiled wide. "I thought it might come to this. So honorable. So righteous." His smile melted. "Would you be so noble if it was someone you loved that was in peril?" He leaned forward, pressing against the cold steel of my blade. A line of red seeped from under its edge.

"Such a pretty little thing, your sister," he said.

"You wouldn't!"

"She's with some acquaintances of mine at the moment. They have been paid to hold her until the Great Door is opened. And if the door isn't opened, well, let's just say that I can't be held responsible for what a group of men like that might decide to do."

I went cold with panic. Was Marcus capable of this? "You're bluffing," I said.

"You think so?" He stared at me, unblinking, his expression unreadable.

"Dear gods, Marcus. Think about what you're doing."

"Just unlock the door, Timothy. Once I'm inside, you can shut it. I'll find my own way out once I know what happened to Therris."

My mind raced. Janice was only twelve. How could he do such a thing? Maybe he was right, and *The Beyond* wasn't what we had believed. Maybe nothing would happen. It would only take a moment to let him in and then shut the door.

"Where is Janice?" I asked, straining to keep the panic out of my voice.

"I promise that she'll be returned unharmed if you unlock the door."

Surprised at my own movements, I sheathed my sword and pushed back the side of my cloak, revealing the brown, leather case on my side. I quickly loosed its buckles and retrieved the large, multi-faceted key. I paused as I beheld my charge, polished to a shine and accented with silver and gold. I couldn't believe I was doing this.

Noting the position of one of the door's brass levers, I selected the proper keyhole and inserted the key. After performing a complex combination of turns and lever pulls, the door whirred to life. The massive gears on its face spun and clicked, levers slid and rose.

The last of the gears came to a stop with a loud clank, and the Great Door fell silent.

Marcus slid his lantern to one side and rushed to the door. Grasping its massive brass handle in both hands, he planted a boot against the cliff. He grunted, pushing with his leg and leaning back. Slowly, the massive door crept open. Once opened enough for him to slip through, Marcus let go.

Still panting from the effort, he scooped up his lantern and held it out before him, staring into the blackness of *The Beyond*. His free hand rested atop his sword's handle. He stood silent for a long moment. Finally, he turned back to face me.

"Thank you. I never wished—"

Marcus's words were choked off with a sickening gag as something resembling a dagger's blade bloomed out of the front of his throat. A large tentacle rose up behind him. Marcus's body shook with the movements of the tentacle, apparently attached to the bloodied tip that had skewered him.

The undulating mass extended back into the darkness of *The Beyond.*

Marcus stood stiff. His whole body quivered as his life's blood cascaded down the front of his neck. The lantern slipped from his grasp, shattering on the cobblestone and sending a whoosh of flame around his feet and up his legs.

With a sickening crack, the tentacle retracted, snatching Marcus off his feet and pulling him backward through the opening. In a blink, he was gone.

All fell silent except for the hiss of oil burning on damp stone. What had I done? I wanted to help Marcus, but knew it was likely too late for him. I knew I should be moving, knew I had to stop that thing from getting out, but I was frozen with fear.

I jumped at a sudden noise, like a large tree limb being snapped. Grotesque sounds of tearing and gnawing came from somewhere just beyond the door.

From what I had already seen, and was now hearing, Marcus had met a terrible end. If that thing came back out… I slid the key out of the lock and took a cautious step forward. I had to shut that door.

Approaching footsteps caused me to pause. I turned. Two Gateway Guards were rushing down the cobblestone road, swords drawn and eyes fixed on the partly opened door silhouetted by the flames.

They halted a few feet away when they noticed me. I placed a finger over my lips to warn them to be silent, but one of them spoke anyway.

"What's going on? Why is the Great Door open?" the man said. The flames illuminated his youthful face and wide-eyed stare.

The words had hardly cleared his lips before an elongated form, moving low to the ground, darted out of *The Beyond*. It looked like a giant centipede, easily twice the length of a man. A single, whip-like tentacle attached to the end of its body snapped back and forth as it rushed the soldiers. The light from the flames glistened off the massive set of blood-drenched pincers at the front of its head. The wide pincers had serrated spikes along their inside edge. Bits of bloodied flesh hung from them.

Before either soldier could react to the threat, it was upon them, snapping its scissor-like pincers around the waist of one and shaking him violently from side to side. The other soldier's leather armor did nothing to prevent the creature's dagger-tipped tentacle from piercing deep into his chest. His knees buckled, and he collapsed in a heap. Blood bubbled from his lips as he exhaled his last.

Everything happened so fast. I knew I had to do something, but seeing the speed and power with which this thing moved, I feared that my efforts would be in vain.

The creature continued shaking the soldier trapped in the powerful pincers of its mandible. His sword flew free, clanging across the stone. The creature reared, lifting its upper body, and the soldier, high into the air. It shuddered for a moment before its pincers snapped fully together. The two halves of the soldier's body fell with a heavy thud, his innards spilling across the ground.

With a mix of horror and anger, I started toward the creature, but something immediately grabbed my right shoulder. Startled, I spun around to face Nathaniel, another of the Gateway Guards.

"What is that thing?" he whispered. His voice quivered in obvious panic.

"I don't know, but we have to do something. If it gets into town, or if more of them come out…" I shook my head. "We can't let that happen. I don't know if we can kill this thing or not, but we have to try."

The light of a lantern bobbed in the distance, and the sound of running footsteps echoed off the high cliff. The creature scuttled toward the approaching footsteps, then froze. In an instant, its color changed from dark brown to a light red that matched the color of the cobblestone road. It blended so perfectly with the stones that it all but disappeared. Those approaching people were running straight toward their doom!

I turned to Nathaniel. "I'm going to try to lure it back through the door. Once I do, shut the door as quickly as you can and barricade it with whatever you can find." I handed him the key to the Great Door. "If I don't come back out, make sure Overseer Losweng gets this."

Nathaniel was staring where the creature waited. I grabbed him by the front of his cloak. "Nathaniel? Did you hear me?"

Nathaniel swallowed hard and nodded, then side-stepped a few feet from the door, keeping his back against the wall.

I grabbed a torch out of a bracket on the cliff face and lit it in the burning puddle of oil.

"Stop! Stay away from the door!" I yelled, waving the torch overhead, trying not only to warn those approaching but to draw the creature's attention as well.

It worked. The creature materialized, returning to its more visible, brown color. It spun toward me, jaws wide. With a hiss, it charged, moving with frightening speed.

I turned and ran through the doorway. A pile of gore lay just inside. Several pieces of bone and cloth protruded from the fresh, bloodied remains. A few wisps of smoke rose from the scorched pants of the dismembered corpse. I leaped over them and kept running, saying a quick prayer for Marcus.

Smooth-faced cliffs rose up on either side as high as the flickering light of my torch allowed me to see. Starting at the threshold of the Great Door and extending into the darkness beyond the edges of my torchlight, lush, ankle-deep grass waved in a warm breeze. The grass on the town's side of the door had long since succumbed to the cold and was now brown and shriveled.

I slid to a stop and spun to face my pursuer. My heart thundered in my ears like a war drum. How was I to defeat such a foe? I thought about hiding, but immediately realized there was no cover here. I just stood there, a feeling of numbness flooding every inch of my body.

The creature rushed through the doorway and headed straight for me, countless legs moving in a rhythmic blur. I steeled myself against the charge.

I waved my torch in front of me, hoping to ward off the attack. The creature seemed not to notice, or care. It didn't slow as it lunged for me. I jumped back and to my left, narrowly escaping the deadly pincers. Without pause, the creature's long tentacle, still wet with the blood of my comrades, snapped forward, straight for my face.

I jerked my head back and spun to the side. The tip of the tentacle missed, but one of the jagged barbs near its base caught the edge of my eye, opening a stinging gash all the way to my ear.

I countered quickly, driving my sword between the creature's glistening, black eyes. A sudden burst of adrenaline flooded me as I realized I had hit my mark. But the hope of victory shattered as my sword's tip glanced harmlessly aside. The beast's exoskeleton was as hard as a stone.

Before I could recover for another strike, the creature lunged with its deadly pincers spread wide. This time, I wasn't fast enough to avoid the attack. Its pincers snapped shut around my chest with the force of a steel trap. I felt, and heard ribs splinter.

My vision blurred from the excruciating pain, and I struggled to draw in a breath. I was only vaguely aware of my sword and torch falling to the ground. In the distance, I heard the thud of the Great Door as it fully closed.

I groped at the vice-like mandible, trying to pry it open, but it wouldn't budge. The creature yanked me off my feet, shaking me from side to side. Bolts of pain exploded through my chest with every movement, and the pressure continued to build. Everything began to grow dark. So this is how it ends for me, I thought.

A white glow appeared on my chest. My moon medallion. It must have been flung out from under my cloak by all the shaking. The creature froze, its black eyes clouding over into a milky white. Its pincers opened wide as it pulled back, arching its head into the air.

I fell onto my side with a gasp, drawing in a painful, but sweet, breath.

The medallion around my neck, though not nearly at its brightest, still glowed with a pale light. Between the medallion's light and the red glow from my sputtering torch a few feet away, I was able to spot my sword. The creature reared higher, emitting a rumbling growl as it waved back and forth.

I had to act now. Pushing through the pain, I scooped up my sword and forced myself to my feet. With both hands, I thrust the sword upward. The blade drove into the creature's soft underbelly, sinking to the hilt. I pulled down on the handle with all my strength, falling to my knees with the effort. The sword sliced eagerly, opening a long, gushing wound.

The creature fell to the ground, rolling and thrashing. A putrid, yellow fluid poured from its wound. The corridor rang with an earsplitting hiss as it pitched and rolled.

I staggered back several steps, sword held out at the ready. After several long moments, it curled into a tight ball and finally went still.

Clutching my side, I ambled over to the torch that, thankfully, was still burning. With great effort, I made my way back to the Great Door. I could feel eyes upon me from every direction and heard scuffling and tapping sounds in the darkness to either side. My skin crawled at the thoughts of more creatures just out of sight, ready to pounce at any moment.

After what felt like an eternity, I stumbled the last few feet to the Great Door. As expected, it was completely closed. Using the butt of my sword, I tapped on the door; twice, in quick succession, a short pause, and then a single tap, the signal for "all clear."

A few moments later, the door slowly opened. I half stepped, and half fell through the opening. Nathaniel, who was there with several other Gateway Guards, caught me before I hit the ground. He stared at me in disbelief, then that typical, crooked grin of his finally spread across his face.

I held my hand out to Nathaniel. He looked puzzled for a moment, then his eyebrows rose in recognition. "Oh," he said, pulling the key from under his cloak and handing it to me.

I gave him a wink and the closest thing to a smile that I could muster under the circumstances. "Thank you," I said.

After taking a few moments to gather my strength, I was able to stand on my own. I turned back to the Great Door, which the guards had just finished closing. By the time I finished locking it, a crowd had gathered, gawking at the blood and gore strewn on the cobblestone. From somewhere among the crowd, I heard a familiar voice. "Timothy!"

Janice pushed her way between two of the guards. She was barefooted and had her white dress gathered up to her knees in both hands. As soon as she spotted me, she broke into a run.

Ignoring the pain in my ribs, I shuffled forward to meet her. I threw my arms around her in a tight hug. She buried her thick head of curly brown hair against my neck and sobbed.

"Are you ok? Did they hurt you?" I asked, placing my hands on her cheeks.

"I'm fine--now," she said, still sobbing. She looked up at me, managing to smile. She was such a strong girl.

The cold rain continued to fall and was growing heavier. I took off my cloak and wrapped it around her. Her eyes were fixed on the death and blood near the door. I caused this. A deep pain of guilt twisted my insides. Gods forgive me.

"Come, little one," I said, gently turning her head away from the gruesome sight. "Let's get you out of this rain."

I had a lot of explaining to do, and though I was sickened by the events of this night, I felt a measure of relief. I now had no doubts about the dangers that lay beyond the Great Door. The Gateway Guards and the Keeper of the Key were as important as our ancestors had led us to believe.

With a new sense of purpose, I guided my little sister back up Fate's Way.

Something's Down There

IT WAS A BEAUTIFUL DAY; warm, but not overly so. A subtle breeze stirred the leaves of the trees on the bank of the lake. Jana breathed in deeply. There was a touch of coolness in the air that hinted at the approaching fall. Soon the leaves would change, ushering in the bitter cold of winter.

"Come with me, mom," Becka said, kicking off her flip-flops and rushing down the grassy bank toward the lake. Their house sat just a few hundred feet from an inlet of Lake Kurry. It made for an amazing view, and her daughter thought there was nothing better than having a lake for a swimming pool. In her back yard, no less.

"You know I don't care for it, sweetie. And I only have a few chapters left," Jana said, holding up the small paperback novel.

"Boring," Becka said, drawing out the word. She giggled and walked into the shallow water at the lake's edge.

Jana smiled, taking a seat on the wooden picnic table. Her husband, David, had made the table himself. He could make anything. It was hard going on without him. It had been just over a year now since his fatal heart attack. Not a day went by that she didn't think of him.

It had been hard on Becka too, but they drew strength from each other and had slowly managed to reclaim a semblance of normalcy in their lives. She didn't know what she would do without her daughter. She was strong, like her father. She had his love for the water, too.

Becka was already well out into the lake. Jana had learned to swim, at David's insistence, but she was far from a good swimmer. She preferred to enjoy the lake from a distance.

Becka waved at her and then rolled forward, leaving just her legs sticking up out of the water. She did a slow pirouette while moving her legs back and forth like a giant pair of scissors. Becka came back upright, wiping water from her eyes and smiling toward her mother.

"Show off," Jana yelled. Becka just laughed and started into a backstroke.

Jana slid the bookmark out of her book as she opened it, laying it out on the table. Within a few moments, she was lost in the drama-filled pages of her novel.

"Mom," Becka shouted. Her voice was not panicked, but there was definitely a concern in her tone.

Jana looked up from her book. Becka was treading water in place, her face down close to the water as if looking at something below.

"Something's down there," Becka said.

Jana placed her bookmark in her book and flipped it closed. She started to ask Becka what she saw, but her words caught in her throat. Becka was gone. The water rippled slightly, where she had been just a moment before.

Jana stalked toward the water, keeping her eyes locked on the spot where Becka had been. It had been a good thirty seconds or longer now with no sign of her daughter. Becka was certainly capable of staying under much longer than that, but her last words had set her nerves on edge. "Something's down there." What had Becka seen?

It had been over a minute now with no sign of her daughter. The water had settled and was calm and smooth. "Becka!" Jana screamed. If this was supposed to be a joke, Jana certainly wasn't laughing. "Becka! This isn't funny."

A cold wave of panic rolled over Jana. Something was wrong. She ran into the water, stepping high as she loped forward. Once the water was knee-deep, she dove forward, swimming as hard as she could.

"Oh, God! No!" Jana pushed herself to swim faster, making for the spot where she had last seen Becka. There was still no sign of her. "Please, no!"

Jana took in a deep breath and plunged under the water. She turned about frantically, straining for any sign of her daughter. Nothing. She swam down further, praying that she would see Becka. Her lungs burned for air, eventually forcing her back up.

Jana popped back to the surface and sucked in a deep breath. She spun around several times, looking for Becka. "Becka!" she shouted. Under she went again. She stayed under as long as she could, hoping desperately to spot her daughter. This couldn't be happening!

Jana's body was numb with panic. She felt dizzy. She broke the surface of the water again, gasping and spinning about. "Becka!" she screamed, her voice breaking into sobs. Warm tears flowed down her cheeks. There was still no sign of her daughter.

Jana sat up with a start, sobbing uncontrollably. It took several minutes before she could stop crying. She just sat there, rocking back and forth in her bed. More nights than not, she relived that terrible moment. The moment when she lost all that she had left in her life.

It had been just over three months now since she lost Becka. It still didn't seem real. The pain, though, was all too real. Not being able to find Becka's body made it even harder to accept. Divers had spent days searching the lake but found no sign of her.

She told the police and the wildlife department that Becka had seen something in the water just before she disappeared. They claimed there were no predators living in Lake Kurry. It was assumed that she simply drowned. Jana was never convinced, and Becka's last words haunted her. She had not been back in the water since that day.

Jana looked over at the clock on her nightstand. It was only 1:20 a.m. She threw the covers off and swung her legs over the edge of the bed. She ran her fingers through her hair, pushing it out of her face. After slipping on her house shoes, she walked, by feel, into her bathroom. She flipped on the lights, wincing at the burst of light.

Jana took a moment to allow her eyes to adjust before walking to the sink. She splashed cold water onto her face, and stood, staring into the mirror. Her eyes were so red and swollen from crying. Her long, brown hair that she used to keep brushed perfectly straight and smooth was now an unkempt mess.

Jana opened the mirrored door and retrieved the prescription bottle. These were supposed to help her sleep and deal with her anxiety. It did little for either. She shook out two of the pills into her hand and tossed them into her mouth, swallowing them dry.

Instead of going back to bed, she turned on the television and curled up on her couch. At some point, several hours later, she managed to find sleep again.

Jana woke to the ringing of her phone. She sat up and rubbed her eyes, not making any effort to get to the phone. It was probably work again. She didn't care.

Finally, the phone stopped ringing. Jana looked up to the clock on the wall. It was almost noon. She sat on the couch for several more minutes, noting how quiet and empty the house felt. She wasn't sure how much longer she could do this, or how much longer she wanted to do this. Not for the first time, she thought about taking her own life.

She quietly shuffled into Becka's room. The bed was neatly made, and all of Becka's books, trophies, posters, and other items remained in their places, just as Becka had left them. Jana hadn't been in Becka's room much since losing her. It was just too painful. Today, for some reason, she felt she needed to.

Jana pulled back the white, wooden chair from in front of the desk and sat down. A jewelry box and an assortment of makeup occupied one side. A metal jewelry stand and a small mirror took up most of the other. A framed picture of Becka, standing between her and David, sat in the center of the desk.

Jana felt a lump rising in her throat as she looked at it. She forced herself to look away.

A dozen or more necklaces and bracelets hung from the silver spokes of the jewelry stand, most of them handmade by Becka. Some were made using beads and trinkets purchased from a nearby craft store, but many incorporated hand-carved bits of wood and colorful stones that Becka had gathered from the lakeshore.

One of the bracelets caught Jana's eye. It was made from blue and yellow cord and had an odd-looking stone fastened into it as the centerpiece. The smooth, round stone was hollow and slightly curved. Its shape reminded Jana of the macaroni in the mac and cheese that Becka so loved. It was nearly clear, but had a slight amber tint.

Jana picked it up. It seemed to soak up the muted sunlight streaming into the room from the window near Becka's bed.

A memory of Becka, on the day she drowned, sprang up. It was Becka, asking her to swim with her as she jogged down to the water. Becka was wearing a necklace with the same colors and a similar stone woven into it.

Jana placed the bracelet onto her wrist, tying it through blurry, tear-filled eyes. She looked again at the picture on the desk. "I miss you so much, Becka," she said. "And your father too. If he had been there for you that day instead of me, maybe he would have gotten to you in time."

The tears flowed freely once again. "I'm so sorry, baby," Jana said. She laid her head on her crossed forearms and bawled.

Jana spent the rest of the day on the couch, holding the framed picture of her family and trying, in vain, to convince herself that she could go on without them.

Jana looked out through the large, living-room window and noticed it had started snowing. She laid the picture down on the couch and walked out onto the porch.

Dusk was settling in, but it was still light enough to see out onto the frozen lake. A thin layer of snow already covered the ice. Her eyes were immediately drawn to the spot where she last saw Becka. It was maybe eighty feet out, roughly halfway between the bank at the edge of their yard and the opposite bank at the edge of a wooded area.

Jana was down the steps and walking across the yard toward the lake before she even thought about what she was doing. The only thing she had on was a t-shirt, pajama pants, and her house shoes. It was frigid outside, and the snow was still falling. She paid no attention to either.

Jana walked straight out onto the lake. The ice held her weight, but it hadn't been frozen over long and was likely not too thick. She marched straight out to the spot where Becka had disappeared. She closed her eyes, remembering how beautiful that day was, how happy and playful Becka had been.

Jana fell onto her knees. "Why?" she screamed up at the darkening sky. She laid flat on her stomach with her face against the snow-covered ice. She would give anything, and everything, to have her family back.

A subtle warming sensation crept into her left wrist. She pulled her arm up in front of her face, not bothering to raise her head from the ice. Maybe she was just imagining it, but the stone in her bracelet seemed to glow with a faint amber light. As she continued staring at the stone, the glow grew brighter, and the warming sensation intensified. It quickly spread into her hand and the lower portion of her arm.

Jana heard a noise from below her and felt a vibration in the ice. She raised her head up. Through a clear spot in the ice where the heat of her face had melted the snow, she caught a flicker of movement. She swiped away a large swath of snow with the edge of her palm and forearm to get a better look.

Just below the surface of the ice, directly below her, a large pair of glowing, yellow eyes stared up at her. Jana let out a shriek and rolled over onto her back. Her heart felt like it was ready to burst out of her chest. She didn't see it clearly but saw enough to tell there was a human-like face framing the eyes. What on earth!

The last words of her daughter sprang to mind. Something's down there. Was this what Becka had seen? Was this what had taken her daughter from her? Her fear was replaced with a rising anger.

Her husband liked to hunt and had several rifles, which she still had. Jana's only thought at that moment was getting one of those guns and exacting revenge on this creature.

Jana shot to her feet and turned to run to her house. With her first step, she slipped, falling hard onto her bottom. The ice instantly gave way under the impact of her fall.

Jana plunged into the icy water. The shock of the bitter cold nearly caused her to gasp in a lung full of water. After she broke the surface, she did gasp. Her whole body shuttered in protest.

She grabbed onto the edge of the ice and tried to pull herself up, but it broke free under her weight, plunging her beneath the water once again. This time, before making for the surface, she took a moment to look around her. She could imagine the mysterious, yellow-eyed creature coming for her.

She hurriedly turned about in all directions, expecting to see the creature at any moment, but saw nothing. It was nearly dark outside now, and what little light remained didn't penetrate through the snow-covered ice. She wouldn't have been able to see anything at all were it not for the faint, amber glow coming from the stone in her bracelet.

Just as Jana was readying to ascend, she spotted something in the distance far below. It was a glow that matched that of the stone on her wrist but was much larger.

Jana broke the surface and took in a deep breath. She shivered uncontrollably as she held onto the icy rim. Her body was going numb. She feared that as soon as she pushed her weight onto the ice, it would just break away again. A calm settled over her at the realization that she didn't care. Let the creature come for her, or let the waters claim her. "I give up," she said.

Jana let go of the ice and slipped into the dark, icy water. As she began to sink, she again saw the glow in the distance. A thought came to her. What if that was what Becka had seen that day and not the yellow-eyed creature?

Jana was resigned to death, but she would see this thing for herself before succumbing to it. It was strange that she would care to satisfy a curiosity when she was in the process of losing her life. But this curiosity may have been the cause of her daughter's drowning.

Jana swam with all her remaining strength, diving for the mysterious glow in the depths below. As she drew closer, the amber glow grew brighter and larger. The stone on her bracelet glowed brighter as well. Her lungs screamed for air, her arms and legs felt so heavy.

She wasn't going to make it. Jana stopped swimming and just floated in the silence, staring at the beautiful glow in the distance. Something large darted in front of the glowing object, its body silhouetted against the amber light behind it. It's upper half looked like a person, and it's lower half, from the waist down, looked like the tail of a massive eel. It undulated back and forth in powerful strokes that propelled it forward and up. It was headed straight for her.

Jana didn't have the strength to flee and knew it would be futile anyway. The creature was closing in on her with incredible speed. She closed her eyes.

The assault that she expected didn't happen. Instead, she felt the slimy skin of the creature as it grabbed hold of her left wrist and yanked her forward and down.

Jana opened her eyes to see that she was speeding toward the glowing object below. Her lungs felt like they were ready to explode. She considered just inhaling the lake water and welcoming the end. For some reason, though, she fought to hang on.

A sliver of light from the stone in her bracelet spilled out between the creature's webbed fingers, but it wasn't enough to see by. As they drew closer to the source of the light below, however, she was able to see her captor clearly.

The creature was larger than she had first thought. It had two, muscular arms with wide webbing between each of its fingers. Its thick, muscular chest was the same gray color as the mud on the lake's banks. Its full head of black hair grew down the back of its neck and extended down the length of its back as well. Its head was oversized, with large slits along either side. It reminded her of a fish's gills.

At last, she was finally able to see the source of the rich, amber light. It was a circular opening in the shelf of mud and rock, easily eight feet in diameter. It appeared to be made from intertwining tubes of crystal that wove in and around each other like a giant wreath. The source of the light seemed to be coming more from whatever was beyond the opening than from the crystal structure itself.

The creature didn't slow. It pulled her closer to its own body, wrapping both arms around her before speeding through the glowing ring.

The moment they passed through the ring of crystals, the water instantly went from freezing to warm. It was suddenly much clearer, as well. Shafts of sunlight penetrated deeply into the water.

Jana looked back at the portal of amber crystals. The creature, still holding her tightly, ripped the bracelet from her wrist, snapping the cord easily. The moment it did so, the glowing, crystal portal vanished. The area where it had just been was now only solid rock and mud.

At last, they broke the surface. Jana heaved in a breath, gulping in the fresh air. She was only vaguely aware of the creature pushing her up onto the bank. A wave of dizziness overtook her, and everything went black.

* * *

"Mom." The voice sounded so faint and distant, but there was no mistaking the sweet voice of her little girl. "Mom. Are you okay?" The voice was much louder and clearer now.

Jana suddenly became aware of the feeling of water on her legs and the tickle of grass on her nose. She opened her eyes, wincing against the light. The sun was bright overhead. She was lying on a blanket of thick, green grass at the edge of a lake of the clearest water she had ever seen.

She stood up, and then heard her daughter's voice again, calling out to her. She spun around to see Becka running down a gently sloping hill. Knee-high flowers of bright reds, yellow, and purple grew thick everywhere.

"Mom," Becka said, continuing to run toward her. "I can't believe you're here."

She couldn't believe her eyes. Becka was here! Jana had no idea where "here" was, but it didn't matter. Becka was wearing the same bright yellow and orange bathing suit that she was wearing the day she drowned.

Becka wrapped her arms around her mother. Jana returned the embrace and started crying, but this time, for the first time in many months, it was tears of joy. If this was a dream, she didn't ever want to wake. A thought suddenly occurred to her.

She held Becka out at arm's length and looked into her beautiful, brown eyes. "I didn't make it did I? Is this heaven?" Jana said.

Becka's brow wrinkled in confusion. "What are you talking about, mom?"

"If I'm here with you, then we must be in heaven?" Jana said, smiling at her daughter.

"Mom, why would we be in heaven? I mean, I hope we end up in heaven together, but don't you have to die first?"

Jana wasn't sure of how to respond to that. Did Becka not remember what had happened? "Baby. Do you not remember what happened to you?"

"What *happened* to me? Mom, you're scaring me. Are you okay?"

"Becka, you drowned over three months ago. You don't remember it?"

"Drowned?" Becka said. Her voice filled with obvious confusion. "Three months ago? I was with you not five minutes ago, mom."

Jana shook her head. None of this made any sense. "Becka, I haven't seen you since that day on the lake back in the summer."

"Back in the summer? Mom, it's still summer," Becka said, gesturing with her hand at the grass and flowers all around them.

Jana's mind reeled. It certainly felt and looked like summer. Had she completely lost it?

"But it's December," Jana said. "I fell through the ice, and that thing brought me here. Through the glowing crystals."

"You saw them too?" Becka said.

Becka spent the next several minutes telling her account of what had happened to her. How she saw an amber-colored glow deep in the water and swam down to see what it was. She saw an opening ringed with glowing crystals, and swam through it. She was immediately surrounded by two of the strange creatures. One of them snatched the necklace from her neck and, just like with her when her bracelet was taken, the portal of glowing crystals immediately disappeared.

Becka then came ashore and set about trying to figure out where she was. She climbed to the top of the hill, taking in the view of the valley below. A noise from the direction of the lake caught her attention, and that's when she saw me laying on the bank at the water's edge.

According to Becka, she hadn't been here for more than a few minutes.

Jana struggled to make sense of what she was hearing. Becka seemed equally taken aback when she told her of all that had transpired since she last saw her, over three months ago, and how that everyone had assumed her dead.

Jana had never believed in the supernatural, to any degree, but yet here she was, united with her daughter. Though neither of them could explain the why and how of it, they both finally came to the conclusion that passing through the glowing portal had brought them to this mysterious place; a place where time apparently passed quite differently than it did in the world they both knew.

"So how do we get back home?" Jana asked, not that she expected Becka to have the answer.

"I don't know. But I know where we should start." Becka took her by the hand and started up the hill.

Once they reached the top, Becka pointed down to the valley stretched out below. It was dotted with dozens of log houses of various sizes and shapes.

Jana had no idea where they were or where they were going, but she had her daughter back. That was enough.

Jana put an arm around Becka and smiled at her. "Well, let's get on down there."

Becka smiled back and nodded.

Like a scene out of a fairy tale, the two of them set off to find their way in a mysterious new world.

The Shadow's Host

PENDRULE AND HIS TWO COMPANIONS slipped into the narrow opening in the massive wall of rock. The last, dying rays of the sun weakly sifted through behind them.

The three walked in silence for nearly an hour, navigating a maze of twisting tunnels as they worked their way deeper and deeper into the depths of the mountain.

"I don't like this place," Krelg said, rubbing his hands together. It was then that he noticed his breath rising as he spoke and how cold it had suddenly become. He wasn't the only one who felt so. Pendrule and Olbreh were pulling their cloaks

about them tighter and rubbing their arms in an attempt to keep warm.

Pendrule raised a fist, and the party halted.

"What is --"

"Shhhh," Pendrule said, wrinkling his brow and cocking his head to the side, apparently listening for something further down the narrow passage. The three stood motionless, the only movement was the flickering dance of flames from Krelg's torch.

Pendrule motioned for him and Olbreh to stay put. He slid his stag-handled dagger from its leather sheath. The unnaturally sharp blade, forged from green-steel, had tasted the flesh of many a foe unfortunate, or foolish, enough to cross Pendrule.

Without a word, Pendrule trotted off into the darkness. His practiced movements were silent and swift. Being a valkin, Pendrule could see as well in complete darkness as the other races could in broad daylight.

As instructed, Krelg and Olbreh remained where they were, though neither liked taking orders from Pendrule. He wasn't even a Defender. They did, however, have orders from Colonel Crauwold to do as Pendrule instructed. Pendrule *was* the one who found the entrance to the lost grave house and, supposedly, knew the way into it.

Grave houses were notoriously dangerous places. Many

were elaborately designed structures resembling homes, complete with living quarters. Others were simple, one-roomed structures. But all were full of traps, intended to protect the owner's hidden treasures, or the owners themselves. True to their name, grave houses often became the final resting place for any that dared enter them.

Krelg admired Pendrule's bravery, and there was no denying his exceptional talent. When it came to slipping around in the shadows, there was no one better. But, despite being Shinkai, Pendrule had refused to join ranks with the Defenders. Why any Shinkai would refuse to stand with others gifted with the ability to wield the Mystic Forces, was beyond his comprehension.

Krelg shook his head, staring into the darkness where Pendrule had vanished. What a waste. With the guidance of the Defenders, Pendrule could be ten times the conjurer that he was now. Krelg, being Shinkai himself, knew this from personal experience. Since enlisting at Fort Algusta, four months earlier, his skill with the Mystic Forces had already grown by leaps and bounds. He now controlled, and could effectively conjure, *Air*, *Fire*, and *Spirit*.

"I just want to confirm this location and get out of here," Olbreh said, keeping his voice low as not to disturb whatever Pendrule had slipped off to investigate.

"Me too," Krelg said. "Something about this place doesn't

feel right."

"Well, we *are* expecting to find a grave house, Krelg," Olbreh said.

Krelg smiled and shook his head in agreement. "Good point," he said.

The two spun in unison toward the dark corridor where Pendrule had disappeared as a single bat fluttered past them. Both sighed in relief and relaxed their grip on their swords.

Grave house or not, the place unsettled Krelg. The air seemed unnaturally cold and heavy. Even the smoke from his torch seemed to struggle to ascend. Something was not right about this place. Not right at all.

"What's keeping Pendrule?" Olbreh said. He shifted from side to side, turning back and forth to ensure no one, or thing, was sneaking up from behind.

* * *

The air had turned significantly colder and was filled with a deep foreboding and sense of dread that Pendrule had felt only one other time in his life; when he had scouted this same area two weeks earlier. It was much stronger this time though. Hungrier.

Pendrule surveyed the darkness, his valkin eyes easily penetrating the inky blackness of the cavern. He could feel the source of the pervading evil. It was close. Hopefully the treasures to be recovered would be worth tangling with

whatever was here.

Two tall doors of aged oak stood proudly, marking the entrance to the grave house. Much of the gray stone to either side of the doors had long since crumbled to fragments on the floor. But remarkably the oak doors still stood, as if in proud defiance of reality. One door remained half open. The thick layer of dust and the curtain of cobwebs draped across the opening suggested that none had ventured here in a very long time.

A soft whisper drifted out of the darkness, just beyond the grave house's entrance. The voice was raspy and dry, yet somehow inviting. "Come to me," it said.

In a blink, Pendrule was drawing upon the Mystic Force of *Fire.* Its radiant warmth cascaded into his body. As the Mystic Force raged into him, so did an eagerness for combat. He held his dagger at the ready in his right hand. His left palm extended out in front of him, fingers spread wide. He mentally prepared to conjure a searing ball of fire that he could unleash the instant it was needed.

"Come to me." The voice- no, not a voice, but a thought, once again called to him from within the ancient ruins.

Still drawing upon *Fire,* Pendrule sliced away the cobwebs and stepped through the opened door. Slowly, and cautiously, he picked his way through the rubble and debris. The air grew colder with each step, yet several beads of sweat still managed

to form on his brow.

"Who are you?" Pendrule said, as much to himself as to his beckoner.

No reply. Nothing stirred in the distance, yet Pendrule was sure he felt the presence of someone, or something, not far ahead. He continued on.

* * *

In the center of a cobblestone courtyard stood a round, stone well. A thick blanket of frost clung to its walls. Once a source of refreshing water, the well was now home to a brooding evil; a dark and soulless entity spawned from the Corruption itself.

It was a host that this entity craved, and with its probing essence, it had found not one, but three such beings who could fulfill its desires. It was the closest one, though, that it desired most. What strength this one held, and a spark of defiance that made him that much more appealing. Yes, he would make a perfect host.

Pendrule would not be the first such victim of the Corruption-spawned entity. Like the others, his body would be used as a means to move about the land, slaying and tormenting for the pure delight it brought. And when Pendrule's body gave in to the cancerous evil and finally died, it would simply move on to someone else.

A near-silent footstep sounded some thirty yards from the

well, but even the stealthiest approach couldn't escape the entity's senses.

Just, a little, closer.

* * *

Pendrule went stiff with shock as the Mystic Force of *Fire* was stripped from his grasp. The backlash from having any of the Mystic Forces pulled away unexpectedly was an intensely painful experience.

The evil that had grown stronger with every step was now upon him. Pendrule scanned the area around him. His eyes locked onto a small stone-walled well. A thin layer of glittering frost clung to its rim and sides. Somehow, he knew that he had found the source of the cold and pervading evil of this place; the very thing he had sensed far back in the main tunnel where he had left Krelg and Olbreh.

Pendrule tried again to draw upon the Mystic Forces, first *Fire*, then *Spirit*; nothing. He could sense them, but trying to embrace them proved impossible. He wasn't sure of what was happening, but he sensed that the culprit resided within the well. He anxiously adjusted his grip on the handle of his dagger. Whatever was capable of severing his connection to the Mystic Forces would surely be a dangerous foe.

Pendrule took a cautious step forward, keeping his eyes locked on the rim of the well. "All right. Come on out and play," he said in a low voice, though in the stillness of the cavern

it seemed to carry forever.

He gave a start when something moved on the top of the well. It looked like a swirling cloud of darkness, only distinguishable from the surrounding black by the small flashes of red dancing within its form.

Pendrule immediately decided this was not a foe he wanted to face. He tried to back away, but his legs wouldn't move. A rare emotion began to rise with Pendrule; panic.

The entity continued to swirl over the surface of the well, continuously changing form. One moment, tall and thin. The next, short and wide. Then it came for him.

A long, snake-like tendril of the unnatural darkness stretched out toward Pendrule. He wanted to move, wanted to shout, anything but stand there like a helpless fool, but his body was no longer his to control.

The tendril of darkness hovered just inches from Pendrule's face. His breath came in labored gasps, and his heart raced out of control.

"So strong and feared in the world of mortals, but you cower in the face of true strength." The thoughts slid from the shadowy extension like blood from a blade. "My fear leaves you powerless, yesss?"

Pendrule's mouth twisted as if to scream, but no sound escaped his lips. His terror could have been no greater as the tendril of darkness reared backwards like a snake preparing to

strike.

* * *

Krelg and Olbreh jumped in unison as a blood-curdling scream echoed through the tunnel from the darkness beyond; a sound of pain and torment that would be commonplace in a torture chamber. They both stared down the tunnel where Pendrule had gone, eyes wide.

Olbreh swallowed hard. "What, in the great beyond, was that?" he said.

Krelg turned to face Olbreh, trying his best to look confident. "Perhaps we should find out," he said. "Be prepared for anything."

Krelg took the torch from Olbreh and started off in the direction of the scream. After a moment's pause, Olbreh exhaled deeply and followed.

* * *

Pendrule walked through the cavern, testing his new legs. An occasional flicker of red danced across his vision. Many of the soulless creature's powers would be limited or useless now, but it had gained many new abilities; the ability to conjure the Mystic Forces, to move about freely, to feel, to kill.

The green-steel dagger flashed forward in a stabbing motion, then recoiled with lightning speed, twirling easily around Pendrule's hand before sliding effortlessly into its sheath. The entity that was now Pendrule, smiled wide before trotting off in the direction of the other two mortals that had entered its home.

Pendrule's mortal mind and thoughts still lingered within his body, but they now belonged to the entity. It tasted them, as if to sense their intent, their purpose. The thoughts that once belonged to Pendrule were now just toys for the entity to play with and destroy at its leisure. One thought slid to the surface and caught the entity's attention. "I must warn General Tirey and the others."

The entity found the thought amusing. "I don't think so. But I do think a visit to this General Tirey could be worth my time." It was Pendrule's mouth that moved, but the voice that came out was dry and raspy, not at all like the smooth, casual tone that belonged to the former valkin.

Pendrule moved swiftly and eagerly along the narrow corridor that led up to the surface, stopping at every side tunnel to *feel* for the two mortals. He yearned for the taste of death with no less intensity than a ravenous wolf craved the tender flesh of a lamb. It had been far too long. He continued through the lightless corridor, the only clue of his presence was the occasional flicker of unnatural red in his eyes.

* * *

Krelg and Olbreh cautiously descended through the

twisting tunnel, occasionally calling for Pendrule as loudly as they dared. Both feared the worst, but neither spoke it, as if avoiding it would somehow make it not so. If the deathly scream they heard was from Pendrule, then surely he must be dead and who, or what, killed him they did not look forward to finding.

The tunnel forked in front of them, with no sign of which way Pendrule had gone. Krelg knelt and examined the floor, holding the torch low and searching for some clue of Pendrule's passing. Nothing. Krelg stood and peered down both tunnels.

"He could have gone either way. The floor is so dry and rocky. I can't make spit of it." Olbreh placed a hand on Krelg's shoulder to ease him. The situation was unsettling, to say the least, but they needed to stay calm and focused.

"Let us choose either one for a distance. If we don't soon see signs of Pendrule, we'll simply try the other. He can't have gone far," Olbreh said.

"A solid plan," Krelg said. He took one last glance down both tunnels before heading to the left, mumbling something to himself. The only words that Olbreh caught were, "Pendrule" and, "sticking together."

The two hadn't gone far before the tunnel stretched open into a wide cavern that was at least a hundred paces wide and just as deep.

"This place is immense," Olbreh said, gazing up at the

rock ceiling far overhead. Huge stalactites hung down like the fangs of some giant creature.

Krelg was already making his way across the expanse, head turning from side to side, surveying the area for any signs of movement, or anything else that could pose a threat. Olbreh followed close behind.

As they approached the far side of the cavern, the sound of dripping water sounded from up ahead. Krelg held the torch out, revealing a large pool of water covering nearly thirty paces of the cavern floor. The water was still except for the ripples caused by the occasional drops of water slipping from the stalactites overhead.

A disturbing thought suddenly came to Krelg. He had heard of places, mostly in underground caverns such as this, where it was not possible to draw upon the Mystic Forces.

Krelg let his senses become receptive to the Mystic Forces. Flows of *Air*, *Fire*, and *Spirit* rushed through him like a hurricane. His body felt lighter than air, so in control, so powerful. Holding the Mystic Forces made him feel safe. He felt as if no one in the world could harm him at that moment.

Of course, drawing on the Mystic Forces did not make one all powerful, but it could make you feel as though you were; a false sense of security that had been the undoing of many a novice Shinkai.

Krelg was aware of such things, and was never one to underestimate any opponent. His ability at conjuring the

Mystic Forces was exceptional, but he knew his limitations and had worked equally hard to hone his skills in physical combat.

After a moment, Krelg released the Mystic Forces. He was completely oblivious to the signal he had just sent out to the creature that was already stalking him and Olbreh. If it didn't know exactly where they were before, it did now.

"I don't think Pendrule came this way," Olbreh said.

"I think you're right. We'll try the other tunnel."

Just as they turned to head back, Olbreh stopped abruptly. He raised his sword in a defensive stance. "Something isn't right. Do you feel it?"

Before Krelg could reply, a tall figure stepped into the edge of the torch's light. In an instant, Krelg seized upon *Fire* and *Spirit*, ready to wield the Mystic Forces as well as his broadsword that he held at the ready. He looked to Olbreh. He gripped his sword in both hands and spread his feet wide, preparing for combat.

The figure continued to approach, walking casually and showing complete disregard for the two, armed Defenders. As the figure stepped fully into the torch light, they immediately realized it was Pendrule.

Both sighed with relief and visibly relaxed, though for some reason Krelg chose to hold on to the Mystic Forces for a moment longer. "Where have you been, and what was that horrible scream...." Krelg's words trailed off as he stared at

Pendrule's eyes. He could have sworn that- yes, there it was again, a flash of red moving within his eyes. Krelg took a step back.

"What's the matter? You don't look well," said Pendrule. His voice was cold, with a harshness that reminded Krelg of a file sliding across steel.

Krelg gave Pendrule a questioning stare. "Answer me. Where have you been?" Krelg knew that something was very wrong. A palpable sense of evil emanated from Pendrule.

Olbreh stepped up to Pendrule and placed a hand on his shoulder. "What is wrong with you Pendrule? Didn't you hear what Krelg jus-"

The words caught in Olbreh's mouth as the long blade of a green-steel dagger slid under his ribs. Reflexively, Olbreh grabbed the dagger that had impaled him, his eyes wide with shock.

Pendrule, or more correctly, the soulless creature that now inhabited his body, wrenched the dagger free. Several of Olbreh's fingers dropped to the floor, then he followed, collapsing to his knees. Blood poured heavily from his mouth, gurgling as he struggled to breathe. Pendrule's lips curled in a devious smile.

Krelg couldn't believe what he was seeing. He stood in numb silence for what felt like an eternity. Time seemed to slow to a crawl.

Krelg blinked, coming to his senses just as Pendrule knocked Olbreh onto his back with a forceful kick to the face. Pendrule stepped over him, dagger twirling and dancing around his hand.

Krelg met Pendrule's cold gaze with a mixture of anger and confusion. "You're mad!" he shouted.

Pendrule responded by lunging forward, slicing at Krelg's throat with a horizontal slash. Krelg was ready. He leaned backwards, easily avoiding the blade. Pendrule pressed on, dagger slicing and darting. Each time, Krelg dodged cleanly or deflected Pendrule's blade with his sword.

Krelg stepped in and feigned a thrust for Pendrule's head, but instead dropped low, sweeping out and forward with his left leg. Both of Pendrule's legs were knocked out from under him, landing him hard onto the stone floor. Krelg spun on around with the momentum of the kick, stopping in a low stance, facing his downed adversary.

Krelg dropped his torch and brought his thumb and fingers together, pointing them at Pendrule. A brilliant flash of silver lightning exploded from his fingertips, illuminating the entire cavern.

Pendrule rolled to the side, narrowly avoiding the bolt of lightning. The lethal energy slammed into the ground with a tremendous crack. Bits of rock and dirt flew in all directions leaving a smoldering hole where Pendrule had fallen.

Pendrule used the momentum of his roll to spin up onto one knee. He came up facing Krelg with one hand extended in front of him. A crackling ball of white-hot fire streaked from his open palm, leaving a long tail of flame to mark its flight.

Krelg dropped into a crouch. The ball of fire singed his hair as it soared past, missing the top of his head by a finger's width. The fireball slammed into the back wall of the cavern, disintegrating into a shower of sparks. The glowing remnants dropped into the water below with a loud hiss and burst of steam.

Krelg wasted no time in seizing the Mystic Forces again. This time he drew upon *Air*, conjuring an invisible shield of solidified air across the front of his left forearm. He lunged forward, slamming the shield into Pendrule's upper chest. The top of the air shield clipped Pendrule's chin, violently snapping his head back.

A lengthy blade of green-steel sunk deep into the invisible barrier right over Krelg's heart. The force of Krelg's momentum knocked Pendrule completely off his feet and sent him sliding across the stone floor on his butt.

Krelg looked down at the blade suspended in the air, its tip just inches from breaking through to his chest. That was close.

The area flickered with dying light as the torch on the floor ate at the last bit of its fuel. Krelg had no desire to fight

Pendrule in complete darkness. That would be suicide. Drawing upon *Fire* and *Spirit*, Krelg conjured again and a sphere of pure light manifested high overhead illuminating the room with a golden glow.

Pendrule leaped back his feet. He wasn't breathing hard at all and paid no attention to the steady drip of blood coming from a deep gash in his chin. He smiled as he stalked toward Krelg.

Krelg released his conjuring of *Air* and the air shield immediately dissipated. He caught Pendrule's dagger as it fell free. Unlike Pendrule, he was breathing hard now, but his concentration remained razor sharp.

Krelg took a step backwards, giving ground to Pendrule. "Why are you doing this, Pendrule? I am not your enemy!" No response. "Don't make me kill you!"

Pendrule laughed loudly. "You? Kill me? You flatter yourself, mortal." The words were so cold and alien. Pendrule was often rude and distant, but nothing like this. And that last thing he said, "Mortal"? Krelg's breath caught at the sudden realization. This was not Pendrule he was fighting; at least, not Pendrule alone.

Krelg set his feet, fully prepared to cut Pendrule down if he came any closer. Pendrule came on, never slowing. A sword of crackling fire burst to life in Pendrule's left hand as he leaped into hand-to-hand combat with Krelg once more.

Swords met again and again. Brilliant, red sparks sprayed into the air with each clash of steel against fire. Krelg felt the burn of fatigue creeping into his muscles. He fought vigorously to hold his ground, but didn't know how much longer he could continue this pace.

Pendrule's intensity never let up in the least. Krelg kept his broadsword and the green-steel dagger whirling and slashing in, diving and thrusting, but Pendrule avoided them with unnatural speed.

This had to end, and soon. Krelg reached deep into his reserves, forcing himself to strike faster. He unleashed a particularly complex series of slashes and thrusts, falling into the combat maneuvers ingrained into him during his training as a Defender.

Pendrule leaned a little too far to his right and Krelg seized the opportunity. The green-steel dagger, Pendrule's own dagger, sunk deep into Pendrule's side. With a twist, Krelg pulled it free and leaped backwards, expecting Pendrule to fall from the obviously fatal wound.

Pendrule looked down at his side. Blood poured from the wound, steam rising from it as it rushed out to meet the cold air of the cavern.

Krelg gasped in disbelief when Pendrule slid the blade of his flaming sword across the wound. Blood and flesh hissed and bubbled under the tremendous heat of the sword, sealing the

wound. If Pendrule felt any pain at all, he showed no signs of it.

Pendrule looked up at Krelg, cocking his head to one side. "That wasn't very nice," he said, and then leaped forward.

This was too much. How was he to beat such an adversary? Krelg's mind raced for an answer. A desperate plan came to him. He didn't have enough energy to continue conjuring for long, but if his plan worked, he would only have to do so twice more. He thought to try it at that moment, but if his conjuring failed, he wanted some distance between Pendrule and himself.

Krelg turned and ran for the water. Its surface shimmered with the golden reflection from the orb above. He hoped that it was deep enough to serve his purpose. Without slowing, Krelg dived in headlong and swam for the middle of the pool.

At no point did Krelg touch, or see, the bottom. Perfect!

Pendrule gave chase right up to the edge of the water but then paused.

Krelg was now in the middle of the pool, doing his best to paddle in place while holding onto both his weapons.

"Come on," he said quietly through gritted teeth.

A ball of fire streaked toward him from Pendrule's outstretched palm. Krelg plunged under the surface. The ball of fire exploded into the water with tremendous force. Water and steam raged high into the air.

Two more searing fireballs followed in quick succession,

pounding the water just above him. Krelg's lungs burned for air, but he stayed under for a few moments longer. Finally, the water grew calm. Krelg could stay under no longer. He broke the surface, sucking in air with a loud gasp.

Pendrule still stood at the water's edge, a look of disgust painted on his face. He leaned forward and released a primal scream, and plunged forward. His flaming sword disappeared just before he hit the water.

The moment that Pendrule jumped, Krelg seized upon *Air*. He held his place, waiting for Pendrule to get out a little farther from the bank, where the water should be well over his head.

Once Pendrule was no more than five feet from him, Krelg conjured *Air* around Pendrule's entire body. Pendrule froze in mid-stroke as if he had been turned to stone and immediately began to sink.

Pendrule never broke eye contact with Krelg, and made not a sound as he slipped under the water.

Krelg shivered, as much from the sight of Pendrule sinking to his death as from the bitter cold of the water. Without wasting another moment, he swam to the bank, still conjuring *Air* to maintain the bind around Pendrule.

Krelg tossed his sword and Pendrule's dagger onto the cavern floor, and then pulled himself up onto the cold stone. He rolled over to face the water, staring at the spot where Pendrule had sunk. He never enjoyed killing, but sometimes it

was simply what had to be done.

Krelg slowly got to his feet then raised an arm toward the water, pointing his fingers to the center of the pool. The cavern exploded to life with the silvery blue flash of conjured lightning. The entire width of the pool lit up as the lightning stabbed into its depths. Krelg thought he could make out Pendrule's body deep below the surface.

Krelg sighed and kneeled to the ground, his whole body shaking. Between the extended fight, and using as much of the Mystic Forces as he had, Krelg was overcome with exhaustion.

Employing a technique recently learned at Fort Algusta, he autonomized the air bind wrapped around Pendrule. That would hold the bind without him having to continue conjuring, at least for a few more minutes. Pendrule was surely dead by now, but he wasn't taking any chances; not after what he had witnessed just moments ago.

Krelg stood and walked over to his fallen comrade. Olbreh lay flat on his back in a pool of his own blood, eyes staring blankly. Krelg ran a hand over Olbreh's face, closing his eyes for eternity. He bowed his head to offer up a prayer to the Garu Sharahn on behalf of his fellow Defender.

* * *

Behind Krelg, a shadowy tendril quietly broke the surface of the water.

* * *

General Tirey was seated in his high-backed chair in front of a polished, oak desk. The walls of his office held several enormous tapestries depicting scenes of battle. Most of the scenes accentuated the stark contrast between the pristine lands of Oryathar and the darkened lands overtaken by the Corruption; a reminder of the constant struggle that the Defenders faced.

The general had just dipped the tip of his writing quill into a bottle of ink when there came a soft rap on the door to his office. Without waiting for a response, the door opened partway, and a young knight stepped in, immediately saluting. General Tirey waved him to ease.

"General Tirey, sir. Knight Krelg Talvnon is here and wishes to speak with you." He paused for just a moment before continuing. "He says that he has information of the highest importance that he must deliver to you in person."

General Tirey casually placed the quill into a holder inlaid with gold. "Knight Krelg, ah yes. Send him in."

The young knight gave a short bow then turned on a heel and marched out.

A few seconds later, a tattered and dirt-covered knight stalked into the room, stopping just short of the general's desk.

General Tirey immediately noticed the failure to salute and

was just about to let Krelg know of it, but something curious caught his attention. The general stared at Krelg's face, studying the unnatural flicker of red in his eyes.

Krelg's lips parted with a fiendish smile. "What's the matter General? You don't look so well."

A Cry For Help

CARL SCRAPED THE BOTTOM of his cup with a plastic spoon, angling into the edges to extract every last bit of chocolate ice cream. He licked the spoon clean then tossed cup and spoon into the trashcan before strolling into the art gallery.

The mall swarmed with people packing their way into the small stores, standing in long lines at the restaurants, and generally rushing about. The art gallery, however, was quite different. It was rarely crowded and was always quiet.

Carl walked straight to the farthest aisle on the right side of the gallery, where the more interesting paintings were. Not that any of them were boring, but some certainly had more to appreciate than others.

One by one, Carl slowly walked past the brass easels and their canvas treasures. Snow-capped mountains, red and gold sand dunes, a log cabin nestled among emerald pine trees. A strange way for a fifteen-year-old to spend his evenings, but Carl could think of few things he enjoyed more than art.

Carl paused in front of a tall picture that hadn't yet been framed. It was strikingly different from the others. Heavy lines of black ink wove a series of odd shapes and patterns. Varying shades of gray filled the gaps between the lines of ink, creating a three-dimensional collage. It was tastefully done, but Carl wasn't the biggest fan of abstract art. Anyone could throw together a bunch of lines and shapes.

Something moved across the surface of the picture. A bug? Carl looked closer. One of the small circles in the picture shifted. He blinked hard and leaned in. The lines, circles and shapes began shifting, twisting, and merging. Carl's eyes went wide with disbelief.

Within a matter of seconds the abstract images came together into a coherent scene. Two elm trees stood tall on either side of a cobblestone walkway that led to a two-story house. A pair of large, oval windows stared from the front of the house over an enormous wooden door. A rusty circle of metal hung in the door's center like a ring in a bull's nose.

A twisted, iron handle at least a foot in length arched from the faded wood.

Carl took a step back and turned to the counter. Mr. Alleth was busy with customers. Carl looked back at the picture. It was once again a collage of random shapes and lines. Was this one of those 3D pictures? He had never seen one quite like it if it was.

Carl waited for Mr. Alleth to finish ringing up the elderly couple at the register.

"Say Mr. Alleth, is that one of those 3D pictures?" Carl said, nodding over his shoulder.

Mr. Alleth, a balding man in his mid-fifties with fine wisps of white hair clinging to his temples, leaned around Carl, peering over the top of his glasses. "That? Oh no, but it kind of looks like one doesn't it? I haven't had time to figure out where to put it yet."

The image had been so clear, so real. What intrigued Carl most, though, was that he was fairly certain he recognized the house. It was in the historic district of Wallerly, about eight miles from his home.

"Where'd you get it from?" Carl said.

"A local man brought it in yesterday." Mr. Alleth rubbed his chin in thought. "Silas Abshire was the name. I'm not a particular fan of abstract art, but this one was different. Figured I'd help out a local artist." He leaned forward and lowered his voice. "I don't think he's entirely with it," Mr. Alleth said, tapping the side of his head. "I felt sorry for him."

"Oh," Carl said, turning his attention back to the picture-- still no house or trees. Did something extraordinary just happen to Carl Spencer? Carl smiled. "See ya Mr. Alleth," he said, already halfway to the door.

"Take care, Carl."

* * *

The bus jerked to a stop at the end of Kettle Lane, in Wallerly. Carl hurried down its steps and started down the sidewalk at a brisk pace. The thrill of this excursion was intoxicating. His mother would kill him if she knew he was skipping out on his piano lessons to go off alone in a strange neighborhood.

Margo was actually his adoptive mother, but she was the only mother he had ever known. He was adopted as an infant and never knew his real parents. She was often over-protective, but he loved her dearly. *What she doesn't know won't hurt her*, he thought. He wasn't about to let this opportunity pass by.

Carl kept trying to remember the details of the house as he approached the corner. Was it really the same as the one he saw in the picture, or was he just imagining it? He glanced at his watch. Just four o'clock, he still had plenty of time. He picked up his pace anyway.

Carl turned the corner and stopped, staring in amazement at the very house he had seen in the picture.

"I knew it," he said. But what did it all mean? And most importantly, what was he going to do about it? Carl had never considered himself brave, and didn't like meeting new people, which was why he was surprised to find himself strolling up to the door of a complete stranger's home.

He gave the door a few gentle taps then stepped back and waited. Several moments passed before a loud click came from the door. It creaked open slowly, one eye peeking through the narrow opening. "Who is it?" a man's voice with a heavy lisp said.

"Carl Spencer, sir," Carl said, trying hard to sound confident. "I saw your picture in the mall. Well...I think it was your picture. Are you Silas Abshire?"

The door opened further, revealing a short man with a thinning head of black and gray hair. His white t-shirt, covered in smears and splatters of a dozen different colors of paint, suggested he was at the right place.

The man wrinkled his brow in obvious concern. "Yes, I'm Silas Abshire. Is there something I can do for you?"

His lisp was terrible, but Carl was able to understand him; if barely. Carl picked at his sweater sleeve, not sure of where to begin.

"Well, I'm not really sure. It's just that, I saw your house in the picture in the mall gallery. I thought that maybe it meant something, so I decided to come here." Silas stared back with a blank expression. "I know it sounds crazy," Carl said.

There was an awkwardly long pause. "Interesting," Silas finally said. "Well, Carl, art speaks to us all in different ways. Please, come in." Silas made a sweeping gesture as he backed out of the doorway. Against his better judgment, Carl went in.

The house was full of antique-looking furniture. A large rug of vibrant red, purple, and gold decorated the center of the first room they passed through. Decorative vases, many as tall as he was, sat against one or more walls of every room. A spiraling, oak staircase ascended to the second floor. An assortment of oil paintings, mostly portraits, covered the wall adjacent to the stairs.

Silas led him down a dimly lit hallway. The walls on both sides were covered with paintings of a wide variety of styles and content, none of them were abstract paintings though. They stepped through an archway into what was obviously Silas's studio.

Several easels, some of them empty and others with half-completed scenes, surrounded a squat table littered with tubes of paint, brushes, and cups. A massive fireplace with a stone hearth blazed in the far wall, logs popping and crackling. An enormous chandelier with dozens of twisted, iron bars hung from the vaulted ceiling.

To one side of the room, on a canvas at least six feet tall and four feet wide, stood a mural of swirling shapes and designs of every color imaginable. It reminded Carl of the picture in the mall, except this one was much larger and done in paint instead of pencil and ink.

"I started that one yesterday," Silas said. "It's odd."

"I think it's nice," Carl lied, turning to Silas.

Silas smiled. "No, I meant the fact that I painted it, and the one in the mall too, for that matter. I've never attempted this kind of art until a few days ago. I woke in the middle of the night with these images in my head and haven't been able to think of much else."

"Oh," Carl said, turning back to the painting. A sobering thought occurred to him. He was miles away from home, in the home of a stranger, and no one knew where he was. And Mr. Alleth had mentioned that Silas wasn't quite normal.

This was a bad idea. Carl started to tell Silas he should be going, but then he heard them; the kids at school. He heard them often--they certainly teased him enough. *"Go on home, momma's boy. You wouldn't want to be late for tea."*

No! There was a reason for what he saw. There was a reason he was here, and he was going to find out what that reason was. Just then, a large circle of green shifted on the canvas. A tingle of excitement and wonder pulled at Carl. He leaned closer. The colors blurred, the shapes stretched and twisted. A stunningly detailed picture of a plain-looking, white house with a white picket fence surrounding it appeared on the canvas. A huge rock stuck up at an angle in the yard. A tall, metal pole with an American flag attached to it protruded from its top.

"How is that possible?" Carl said.

Silas stepped closer to Carl. "Excuse me?"

The images seemed to pull at Carl. It almost felt as if he were *in* the painting.

"Carl?"

Carl jumped when Silas placed a hand on his shoulder, but he didn't take his eyes off the painting. "You don't see the house?"

"No," Silas said. "I don't."

Carl described the scene before him in detail. Silas quietly listened.

As soon as Carl described the rock and the flagpole, he heard Silas gasp. He started to ask Carl what was wrong, but his words froze in his mouth as he noticed the flag on the pole moving. It lifted, as if by the wind, and began to wave and ripple.

Carl felt a breeze. The brown leaves in the yard started swirling and rustling. He reached out and touched the metal

pole supporting the flag. It was cold. Carl walked up to the door of the house and turned the knob. It wasn't locked.

"Someone. Please help me!" the pleading voice, a woman's voice, called from somewhere within the house.

Carl's heart went into overdrive. A chill slithered down his back. The voice pulled at him to his core. He felt an instant and inexplicable connection to whoever this woman was. He had to help her.

Carl slowly stepped through the doorway, looking around nervously. The woman's voice called out again. "Somebody, please!" She sounded so desperate.

Carl made his way through the house, following the pleas for help. "Where are you?" he called out.

"Please hurry," the woman cried.

The voice seemed to be coming from behind the door at the end of the hall. Carl rushed to the door and flung it open. Concrete steps led down a steep, narrow passage. A single light bulb hung from the ceiling near the bottom, illuminating a heavy wooden door secured with a deadbolt.

Carl descended the steps. It was quiet now. The only sound was his footsteps. He slowly reached out for the deadbolt.

The door pulled away from him, retreating in a rush of color. The house, then the yard followed. The multi-colored painting snapped into view in front of him.

"Are you ok?" Silas said, turning Carl around by the arm. "You've been staring at that painting for over five minutes. I couldn't get you to respond."

"I...I'm fine. I think," Carl said. He turned back to the painting. The house and yard were gone. He shivered as he recalled the panic in the woman's voice. If he had been quicker, maybe he could have gotten to her.

Carl told Silas what he had experienced. How he had actually been in the house, following the woman's voice. Silas seemed to take it all in with an unusual calm. "Did you really see all that?" he asked.

"Yeah, I did. That woman needs our help." Carl realized how foolish he must sound, but he didn't care. "I know you think I'm probably hallucinating or something, but I have to find her."

Silas's face grew pale. His brow wrinkled, and a haunting, far-away look filled his eyes.

"Silas?"

"I just don't understand," Silas said, his lisping voice barely a whisper.

"Me either," Carl confessed. "But we have to do something."

Silas stared at the floor, slowly shaking his head.

"So you don't think I'm crazy?" Carl said.

Silas didn't respond right away. He ran a hand over his hair and sighed. Finally, he looked up. "I know the place you saw in

the painting. It's the neighborhood where I grew up. That house with the rock in the yard with the flagpole in it; that's Eugene Garrett's house."

Carl didn't recognize the name. He just nodded his head, waiting for Silas to continue.

"He had a daughter my age. We were real close." Silas paused and swallowed hard. Were those tears in his eyes?

"One night, she didn't come home. We had been together in the park late that same evening. She was fine when I left." Silas paused for a long moment, clearly lost in a distant memory. "I never saw her again."

Silas wiped the tears from his face before continuing. "Her father, Eugene, blamed me for her disappearance. He said it was my fault for not seeing her safely home. That man hates me to this day, and probably with good cause. I should have walked her home."

Carl wanted to say something comforting, but all that came out was, "I'm sorry."

"Silas," Carl said, his voice louder than he intended. "You said you know where this house is. Can you take us there?"

Silas held up his hands in objection. "I don't think that's a good idea."

"Surely you don't think all of this is just coincidence? The picture in the mall leading me to your house, your painting here showing me Eugene's house. Someone needs our help, Silas. Eugene's wife may be hurt or dying. We have to help."

Silas stared into Carl's eyes for a long moment before finally nodding in agreement.

* * *

The sense of deja vu was incredible. The rock in the yard, the flagpole, the house itself; it was all exactly the same. Carl knocked on the door of the aged, white house for the second time. This time for real. Silas appeared ready to run. Carl leaned his ear against the door.

"We shouldn't be here," Silas whispered, shifting from foot to foot.

"Shhh," Carl said, putting a finger to his lips. He listened for a moment longer before jerking upright. "I hear someone yelling for help!"

Carl flung the door open and rushed into the house. He had no idea if anyone, aside from the pleading woman, was home or not, but that was unimportant at the moment.

The inside of the house, down to the tiniest detail, was exactly as he had seen it in the painting. Carl raced down the familiar hall. Silas followed close behind. A muffled cry for help sounded ahead, behind the closed door at the end of the hall.

Carl didn't pause when he reached the door. He threw it open and headed straight down the concrete steps, his way lit

by the expected light bulb overhead. Silas stopped halfway down, wringing his hands.

Carl grabbed the deadbolt and slid it back, then pulled the door open. Dull, yellow light spilled into the stairway. Behind the door was a cramped room with a low ceiling of thick, wooden beams and unpainted, block walls. The only furnishings were a small wooden table with a lamp, a large metal tub, and a couch with ripped cushions; all sitting on a dirt floor.

A woman with a tangle of long, brown hair huddled against the far wall, her filthy dress clinched in her fists and pulled tightly against her chest. Dark circles hung beneath her eyes. Her face was dirty and gaunt.

The woman shot to her feet when she saw Carl. "Please help me!" she said, her voice quivering with fear. She peered past Carl to the stairs behind him. "We have to go before he comes back." Carl noticed her bare feet as she padded over to him.

"April?" came a lisping voice from behind. Silas shouldered past Carl to stand before the woman. "Is that you?"

"Silas," she said, tears welling up in her eyes.

"I can't believe it. Is it really you?" Silas said. "But...you..."

"My monster of a father," she said through gritted teeth. "I don't have time to explain now. We have--." Her eyes widened in terror at something behind them.

Carl turned just in time see a man leap down the steps, swinging a wooden baseball bat. Silas managed to duck out of the way, but Carl wasn't as quick. The bat grazed the top of his head. It wasn't a flush hit, but it was enough to send him sprawling to the ground.

Carl fought to clear his vision, pushing himself back to his feet. The ringing in his ears slowly gave way to the sounds of struggle.

A brawny man with a shaved head held Silas from behind, pulling the bat against his throat with both hands. Silas clawed at the bat, kicking wildly. The woman was beating the attacker with her fists, with no effect.

Carl staggered to the table and grabbed the lamp, ripping the cord free and dropping a blanket of darkness over the room. The light from the stairs outside illuminated the doorway just enough for him to make out the attacker.

Carl brought the lamp down with all his strength, connecting squarely on the side of the man's head and dropping him in a crumpled heap. Silas sucked in a breath and fell to his knees.

Carl stared down at the unconscious man, his vision finally clearing and beginning to adjust to the dim light. The man had a strong jawline and sported a gray goatee. He looked strangely familiar; disturbingly so, yet Carl was certain he'd never seen the man before.

Carl turned to Silas. The room spun in a sickening blur. He took a second to steady himself against the wall before helping Silas to his feet. His head was pounding.

The woman kneeled and grabbed the unconscious man under his arms. Leaning back, she dragged him into the room with a few short pulls. After he was inside, she shut the door and slammed the deadbolt into place. With her back against the door, she slowly slid to the floor. She covered her face with both hands and sobbed uncontrollably.

* * *

As soon as they were outside, Carl called 911 on his cell phone.

"Come on. We can wait in my car," Silas said.

Within a few minutes, several police cars and an ambulance came racing down the street, lights flashing and sirens blasting.

The explanation the woman, April, gave the police of what she had been through was a nightmarish revelation. Apparently, Eugene Garret was her father and had been holding her captive in their cellar for the last fifteen years.

Carl wished he hadn't heard many of the things she detailed. He couldn't imagine how someone could do that to another person, let alone their own child.

Carl's thoughts drifted back to the painting. "Why me?"

he said in a near whisper. Silas and April were neighbors, as well as old friends, but what was his purpose in all of this? He couldn't shake the feeling that he was overlooking something.

Perhaps these events were all to reveal a special gift he possessed. Maybe he would see more things in other paintings. Maybe, just maybe, it was Carl Spencer's destiny to help those that others could not.

Carl shrugged and flipped open his cell phone. He had better call his mom.

Lady Death

THARUN SAT ALONE at a round wooden table in the common room of the Golden Pedal Inn, staring at the silver pendant in the palm of his hand. He ran a thumb over the raised images on the polished, silver surface. Flying birds surrounded by twisted vines dotted with leaves and flowers of various shapes. Hopefully, Taisha would accept it; would accept *him*.

He ran his fingers through his tangle of thick, black hair, sighing as he thought of what he had left behind. He had been gone for almost eight weeks now, not a day of which he did not sorely miss Taisha, and regret leaving. He had been a fool, and it was his foolish pride that had taken him this long to return to Blundale.

A chorus of excited murmurs brought Tharun's attention back to the common room. A tall, slender woman accompanied by two muscular men was taking a seat at a table on the far side of the room. She moved with a practiced grace, flowing into the chair like a silk dress in a breeze. Her gray cloak, the color of a storm cloud, was pulled tightly around her thin frame. Long, snow-white hair spilled out from under the hood, which was pulled low enough to hide her face.

Both men wore dull, brown shirts with matching breeches tucked into dust-covered, black boots. Both had sheathed swords hanging from their belts. They eyed the room suspiciously, as if expecting trouble.

"It's her. Lady Death," a patron at a nearby table whispered.

Her title, though not truly accurate, was fitting. Her proper name was Lady Merthus, and she was well known throughout Blundale, and throughout most of the northern lands for that matter, for her ability to see the when and how of one's death. If their time was close at hand, and she was near them, she could sense it. A disturbing gift that often drew unwanted attention. Lady Merthus had made it known that she took no pleasure in the knowledge her gift imparted.

Lady Merthus casually threw back her hood. She was at least sixty years old, though she appeared to be no more than thirty, and was beautiful for a woman of any age. Tharun was not convinced it was her supernatural abilities that earned her the most attention.

Tharun took a last look at the silver pendant before pushing it into his pocket. As he stood to leave, he glanced at Lady Merthus's table, and froze in place. Lady Merthus was staring at him. Her icy blue eyes locked onto his. An expression of grief and horror washed over her face. The sadness in her eyes was unmistakable. She abruptly turned away, feigning interest in adjusting her cloak.

Tharun stood motionless for what seemed like an eternity, heart pounding and wrapped in a cloak of panic. He had to know. Trembling, he slowly crossed the room to her table.

"You saw something, didn't you?" He strained to keep his voice from cracking.

"Yes," came the simple reply as Lady Merthus looked up at him.

Tharun felt like someone had poured a bucket of ice water over him. This couldn't be happening. His stomach twisted, threatening to empty. "How?" he asked.

"You will drown," Lady Merthus said. The sympathetic tone of her voice belied her chilling proclamation.

The knot in Tharun's stomach tightened. He tried his best to dismiss the gruesome images of his own death.

"When?" He swallowed hard, bracing for her reply.

Without hesitation, Lady Merthus answered, "Today."

Tharun's legs nearly gave out. "This can't be," he whispered. Without another word, he turned and made for the door. He had to get to Taisha.

Outside, Tharun shuttered, exhaling deeply. His breath floated away into the crisp morning air. So many things raced through his mind. So much he wanted to do, to accomplish, and now the last moments of his life were falling away like sand in an hourglass.

He set out at a brisk pace, heading down the dirt road that led out of Blundale. His pulse spiked and his breathing quickened when the log bridge that spanned the small river that all but surrounded Blundale came into view. If he wanted to get to Taisha any time soon, he would have to cross it.

Tharun paused a dozen paces from the end of the bridge. There were no obvious signs of weakness or issues, but that did little to calm him. His legs quivered as he looked to the river, some thirty feet below. Lady Merthus's words kept repeating in his head. If her prediction was accurate, and her predictions always were, then this could very well be where he would meet his fate.

After much consideration, Tharun decided against using the bridge. The bridge was the obvious choice, but if he did the unexpected, maybe he could avoid his fate. It was a fool's hope, but he was desperate.

Tharun carefully made his way down the embankment into a knee-deep section of the river. He gasped in a breath between pursed lips as he entered the frigid water, trembling with fear as much as from the cold. He focused his thoughts on Taisha and pushed on. Slowly, and carefully, he made his way toward the other side.

As expected, the water got deeper as he neared the center of the river. At one point it reached the top of his chest. He kept putting one foot in front of the other, placing each step with care while constantly scanning the water for threats.

He could hardly believe it when the grassy bank of the other side came within reach. He scrambled out of the water and up the steep embankment, remaining on all fours until he was well onto solid ground.

With a sigh of relief, Tharun put the river behind him. Could Lady Merthus have been wrong? With renewed hope he raced on, taking a shortcut across Fedder's Meadow.

Soon he was walking alongside a long row of hedges on the outskirts of Halmish, the village where Taisha was born and raised. His dark-green breeches were soaked from the knee down and, like his tattered gray tunic, were now covered with thickleweed burrs; not quite the impression he was hoping to make, but at this point he was just glad to be alive.

There were no more bodies of water between here and Taisha's home. He didn't know how, but he had beaten Lady Merthus's prediction.

"Watch out!" someone shouted from up ahead. A shirtless man with tanned skin, wrinkled like old leather from too much time in the sun, dropped the large pair of shears he was holding. He frantically waved his arms, pointing to the hedges to Tharun's left.

Tharun turned to see a serpentine creature hanging from the hedges by its hind legs. Fine, bronze-colored scales glimmered in the sun. A long, curved tail tipped with a glistening stinger loomed over its head. Before he could jump back, it leaped onto his arm. Claws, teeth and stinger sunk into his flesh.

Tharun growled in pain through gritted teeth, ripping the creature from his arm and slinging it into the hedges. Blood trickled from the multiple scratches and punctures. It felt as if fire were racing through his veins, burning its way up his arm and into his chest.

The man ran to Tharun. "Was that what I thought it was?" he said, staring at Tharun with wide eyes.

"I think it was a scorpion lizard," Tharun said, gritting his teeth through the excruciating pain working its way into his chest. "They're venomous, I think."

The man's voice was full of pity, but he didn't dance around the truth. "They are." He paused for just a moment. Fatally so," he said. He made a gesture of blessing across his forehead and then placed a hand on Tharun's shoulder. "I'm sorry, young man."

"What will happen? I mean, what are the effects of their venom?" Tharun said. He had managed to escape Lady Merthus's prophecy only to have this happen?

"Your lungs will soon fill with fluid, essentially drowning you," the man said.

The words of Lady Merthus, *Lady Death,* echoed in Tharun's head. "No!" He pushed the man aside and ran for Taisha's house.

* * *

Taisha was kneeling in a small flowerbed framed by smooth stones when Tharun stumbled into the yard. Thick beads of sweat dotted his forehead, and his skin had turned a sickly, gray color.

"I'm sorry," Tharun said. His words bubbled forth like water spilling over rocks. White foam clung to the corners of his mouth. Taisha noticed him just then. She dropped her trowel and sprang to her feet, immediately running to him.

He tried once more to speak, to tell her what a fool he had been; to tell her he loved her, but all that came out was a sickening gurgle. With a trembling hand he reached for her, polished silver shown between his fingers.

"Tharun! What happened?" Taisha's voice was filled with panic.

His legs gave out, and he collapsed into Taisha's arms. She held to him tightly, gently lowering him to the ground.

"Tharun, please," she said, sobbing in great heaves.

Tharun stared into her tear-filled eyes and breathed his last.

The Dreamstone

JONITH BACKED OUT OF THE WAY as the three horses galloped into the Melnar Estate stables. A thick cloud of dust rolled in behind them. He coughed and fanned at the dust as he trotted up to the three men, already dismounting.

Jonith didn't know the two men with Korven by name, though he had seen them at the estate often as of late. One of the men, dressed in dark brown pants tucked into a pair of black riding boots and wearing a burnt orange shirt, threw his reins at Jonith, hitting him in the face. "See that you wipe him down good before you put him up," he said. The man stared at Jonith with obvious contempt, his gaze lingering a moment on Jonith's right eye.

A birth defect that had become progressively more pronounced over the years, the lower eyelid of Jonith's right eye drooped, exposing his eyeball to the extent that it appeared ready to fall out of his face at any moment. A mass of thick, red veins meandered across the underside of his protruding eyeball, heightening the grotesque appearance.

Jonith dropped his head. "Yes, sir," he said. He was used to being stared at, but he still didn't like it. The man chuckled as he walked past.

Korven Melnar, master of the Melnar Estate, began pulling off his riding gloves, loosening one finger at a time. He looked very much the part of a lord in his tan riding pants and polished black boots that came up nearly to his knees. His white shirt sported billowing ruffles at the wrists and a high collar that accentuated his strong jaw line.

The third man tossed his reins at Jonith too. Jonith kept his head down, avoiding making eye contact with any of them. The man looked over to Korven and pointed at Jonith with a thumb as he spoke. "Really, Korven, I don't understand why you allow his type to work here. He's going to run off all the women with that face of his." The man gave a fake shiver of disgust before walking away.

Korven wheeled on the man, fixing him with a look of indignation. "Shut up, Tolvey," he said. "Jonith is my…" The words hung in Korven's mouth, his expression changing to one of confusion. Korven turned and marched up to Jonith.

"Yes, Master Melnar?" Jonith said, daring to look up.

A troubled look settled over Korven's face. He stared at Jonith in silence for an uncomfortably long time, and then shoved Jonith hard, knocking him off his feet. "Out of my way, freak," Korven said.

Korven's two companions laughed, falling in beside him as they strode from the stables, taking up a conversation about some of the local women.

Korven glanced over his shoulder at Jonith just before he turned the corner. Jonith couldn't decide if the look on Korven's face was anger or sadness.

Jonith picked himself up off the ground, staring after Korven. He rubbed the small, smooth stone in his pocket. He found it hard to believe that Korven had been a childhood friend. Jonith missed that friendship. After Korven's father had died and left him the family fortune, and the estate, he had changed. Money and power did that to people, apparently.

"He started to call me his friend," Jonith whispered to himself. He knew that Korven would never admit to such a thing, even if it were true. Jonith strongly suspected, and desperately hoped, that he knew the source of Korven's unexpected outburst; the dreamstone.

Jonith pulled the small, azure stone from his pocket and held it up between his finger and thumb. The light danced and played off its surface. It had cost him nearly six month's earnings, but it was money well spent. If the stone really could turn dreams into reality, to any extent… He smiled at the possibilities.

Last night had been Jonith's first attempt at using the dreamstone. Only a small dream to start with, just to test the water. He had no intention of disregarding the mystic's warnings about the stone.

The consequences of losing or breaking it weighed heavily on his mind. He shuttered at the thought of losing his mind and abilities to the stone. Not only that, but every dream experienced while using a dreamstone had the potential to snare the user, forever trapping them in the dream. The consciousness would live on, but the body would remain asleep and eventually die.

Jonith wasn't overly concerned, though. His skill at dreaming was far beyond that of the average person. For as long as he could remember, he had always had the most vivid dreams. He could recall, in great detail, every dream he had each night.

It had only been in the last year, however, that Jonith realized that he could tailor his dreams to his liking. In his dreams, people liked him and respected him. In his dreams, he looked normal. And in his dreams last night, he and Korven were friends again.

Jonith whistled a lighthearted tune as he picked up a shovel and started in on his work.

Several hours, and a dozen stalls later, Jonith knuckled the small of his back. His thin, leather shoes were caked with horse manure, and he was covered in sweat-laden dust.

He walked out of the stables and into the fading light. He would have to hurry if he was going to make it home before it got completely dark.

Jonith made his way down the winding dirt road, the colorful cobblestone paths and sculpted hedges of the Melnar Estate now far behind him. He glanced nervously from side to side, jumping at every sound from the thick woods that hugged the road on each side.

Jonith stopped abruptly when a tall figure appeared on the road just ahead. He held his breath when they started walking toward him. It was a lean man with a beak of a nose set in a long, thin face that hadn't seen a razor in several days. Dark hair hung past his wide shoulders. His gray, wool cloak hung to his ankles, no doubt concealing a weapon.

Jonith glanced about, looking for the best route of escape, but before he bolted, the man spoke. "Mystic Tershia wishes to speak with you," the man said in a gravelly voice. "She says it is urgent, and bids you return with me." Without waiting for a response, the man turned and walked off the road and into the woods.

All Jonith wanted was to go home and lose himself in his dreams. What could Mystic Tershia possibly want with him? What harm might she, or this stranger, bring upon him if he ignored her summons? He thought it best not to find out and rushed to catch up to her messenger.

Jonith hesitantly followed the man, weaving through the trees and brambles of the shadowy forest. Both walked in silence to the log house nestled deep in the woods where Mystic Tershia lived. The soft, yellow glow from several lanterns spilled out of the open door of the house. The man waved a hand toward the door, motioning for Jonith to enter.

Dozens of clay jars of various shapes and colors filled the wooden shelves that lined the walls of the small room. A fire crackled and popped in the hearth. A heavy iron pot hung in its flames. Thick, yellow smoke billowed over its rim, filling the room with an acrid stench.

Mystic Tershia, a short, portly woman of middle age, stood beside a cluttered table in the center of the room. She carefully deposited a handful of glowing pink seeds into a jar before securing its lid and placing it on a shelf.

"Korven Melnar summoned me to his estate today," she said, wiping her hands on the front of her dark brown dress. "He suspects that he has become the target of some sort of spell. He was quite concerned."

Tershia casually turned to face Jonith. A look of pity filled her eyes as she spoke. "I told him that you purchased a dreamstone from me, but that I knew nothing of your intentions, which is true enough. I like you, Jonith, I really do. But I couldn't lie to him. I simply couldn't risk it."

Tershia's eyes narrowed, and her features hardened. "He means you ill, Jonith. I would advise against returning to the estate."

Tershia stepped around the table and gently placed a hand on Jonith's shoulder. "I know you have a kind heart, Jonith, and I know that you would have others see you for who you truly are. I can only imagine the dreams that you have begun feeding the stone. I would hate to see such dreams destroyed. Even if he doesn't destroy the dreamstone, I am certain that he won't allow you to keep it. In either case, all the emotions, hopes, and dreams you have fed the stone will be stripped from you. Take the stone and leave while you still can."

Jonith had yet to put much of anything into the stone, though that hardly changed the current situation. He stared at

Tershia, not knowing what to say. He had no family. Where would he go?

"He w...wouldn't do that," Jonith said, stumbling through his words, words that he realized weren't true even as he spoke them. Korven was no longer his friend. He hadn't been for many years. He doubted Korven was truly anyone's friend. As much as he didn't want to believe it, he knew Korven would come for him, and would likely beat him senseless, or worse.

The mystic's words hung over Jonith like an executioner's axe. Fear twisted his stomach as he thought about what Korven might do to him. He was so tired of being afraid. He wiped a tear from his cheek with the back of his thumb. "Thank you for the warning, Mystic Tershia," Jonith said, bowing. Without pause, he turned for the door and walked away.

Spurred on by the encroaching darkness, Jonith ran most of the way back to his hovel, occasionally slowing to catch his breath. He was grateful for the small amount of light the half-moon provided this night. He breathed a sigh of relief when the silhouette of his house finally came into view.

After lighting a candle, Jonith shed his filthy clothes. With trembling hands, he poured water from a pitcher into a chipped, crockery bowl. He scooped water onto his face with both hands then patted dry with a towel before plopping down on the side of his bed.

Jonith stared at the dreamstone, running his thumb back and forth over its smooth surface, lost in his thoughts.

The candle was little more than a nub when he finally leaned over and blew out the candle. He laid flat on his back and placed the dreamstone on his forehead. He took a deep breath and closed his eyes. His breathing soon slowed, coming in long steady pulls as he drifted away from the waking world and into a world of his own making.

* * *

Jonith woke at dawn and immediately began getting dressed. With shaking hands, he pulled on his shoes. He paused for a long moment, staring at the dreamstone before sticking it into his pants pocket. He retrieved an aged, leather pack from under his bed and what few other belongings he had and stuffed them into the pack. Once outside, he took one last look at his house. With a sigh, he turned and set out for the Melnar Estate.

After the hour-long walk, Jonith arrived at the stables. The morning sun stabbed through the entryway of the stables, highlighting the floating dust particles. He wasted no time starting in on his work, tossing hay into each of the horses' stalls with a long pitchfork.

Jonith leaned the pitchfork against the door of an empty stall. It was still early, but the temperature was climbing fast. He wiped sweat from his brow with the back of his forearm and pulled the dreamstone from his pocket.

He tried to keep his mind occupied by concentrating on his work, but his nerves were starting to get the better of him. He swallowed hard as he fought down the urge to vomit. Jonith squeezed the dreamstone tight in his fist and stood a little straighter. No more being afraid.

Jonith returned the stone to his pocket and pulled open a burlap sack. He measured out the proper amount of cracked corn with a large metal scoop and turned to pour it into the wooden feed trough of the first of fifty horses that had to be tended to.

He jumped with a yelp, spilling most of the feed onto the ground. Korven stood not five feet away, teeth clenched, holding the pitchfork in both hands. He wore a tight-fitting red vest with no shirt underneath. He always enjoyed showing off his muscled physique. Twin, red stripes ran down the outside of each leg of his black pants.

Jonith backed up as Korven walked toward him. The rough planks of a stall against his back brought him to an abrupt stop. He dropped the scoop and held up both hands, patting the air as if to ward off Korven's fury.

"You dare use magic on me?" Korven shouted. "You think to bend my mind to suit your perverted desires?" Korven's face glowed with rage and spit flew from his mouth as he spoke. Jonith thought to say that he had only wanted Korven to like him again, to be friends as they once were, but decided it best to say nothing.

Korven drove the handle of the pitchfork into Jonith's stomach, dropping him to his knees. Jonith doubled over in pain, coughing and gasping for breath.

"I gave you work here at my estate. A kindness that I now see was undeserving. You are a miserable, self-serving wretch." Korven kicked Jonith in the face with such force that Jonith was thrown back against the wooden planks of the stall at his back. A startled horse leaped sideways and began pacing nervously within the stall.

Jonith fell over onto his side, holding a hand over his split lip. Blood spilled between his fingers onto the ground.

"Korven, please—," Jonith began when a powerful kick to the side of his chest drove the air from his lungs.

Using the heel of his boot, Korven shoved Jonith onto his back, and planted the blades of the pitchfork against Jonith's throat. "It's Master Melnar," Korven corrected. "Give me the stone, Jonith," Korven said, a threatening calm returning to his voice.

Jonith immediately produced the dreamstone, holding it out in a trembling hand.

Korven snatched the stone from Jonith's hand and tossed the pitchfork to the ground. He eyed the mysterious stone with a devious smile. "What foolishness have you dreamed into this witch's stone?" he asked, seemingly more to himself than to Jonith.

"Please, Master Melnar. It's all I have," Jonith said. He looked up at Korven and put on his most pleading expression. "All of my hopes and dreams," he said softly.

Korven threw his head back and laughed. "So touching, Jonith," he said. "Maybe I'll enjoy a dream or two with your precious stone before I destroy it."

Jonith lowered his head. "I beg of you, Master Melnar, don't do that."

"I'll do as I please," Korven said, his voice rising to a near shout. He turned and walked away. At the entryway, he paused and then turned back toward Jonith. "You're done here. If you ever set foot on my estate again, I will see you hanged."

Korven tossed the dreamstone up in the air and caught it, giving Jonith a wink before strolling out of the stables.

Wincing at the pain in his ribs and his split and swollen upper lip, Jonith slowly picked himself up. A torrent of emotions welled up within him and then, just as quickly as they came, they began drifting away. It was working! With each passing moment, Jonith felt his fears and anxieties melting away. Along with the stone, they too were becoming distant.

Jonith almost felt pity for Korven should he attempt to use the stone. The hellish torments, fears and self-loathing he would experience from it would be a nightmare he would not likely escape. Jonith himself, in his efforts to construct the most intense and vivid nightmare he could, one that included his worst mental agonies and fears, had only narrowly escaped being snared by the dreamstone. Had he not been so gifted with the ways of dreams, he was certain he would not have.

Whether Korven used the dreamstone, or simply destroyed it, really made no difference to Jonith. Either way, he was free and forever changed.

Jonith saddled up the finest horse in the stables, Korven's horse, before retrieving his leather pack from the tool room. He stuffed his pack into one of the saddlebags, and confidently swung up into the saddle. He spurred the chestnut stallion into a gallop.

Jonith didn't look back as he left the Melnar Estate, and his personal demons, far behind.

Spirit Warrior

DREYOS HARFLINK, FAST BECOMING RENOWNED for his exceptional fighting skills, stooped down to rest at the base of a twisted birch tree. He reached into the pocket of his well-worn leather coat and retrieved a chunk of dried beef. It was tough, and had about as much flavor as a piece of boot leather, but it was food. When was the last time he had sat down to a warm meal?

He had traveled nearly non-stop over the last two months without visiting the first city or town. He had stumbled across a few villages over the course of his travels, but the food they offered wasn't much better than that of which he had been making do. He always accepted their hospitality with kindness, and didn't complain when what they offered him for food looked entirely too much like something he had scraped off his boot the night before. He just closed his eyes and swallowed it as quickly as possible.

Dreyos thought back to the meals he had enjoyed before leaving home. The lovingly prepared meals which his mother, Yora, made. Fluffy, golden bread rolls, boiled sweet corn, roast lamb, fresh summer peas. His mouth watered at the thought.

Dreyos left home two years ago, after a fight with his father, Graylin, and hasn't been back since. He often thought of returning home, to see his mother if nothing else, but his stubborn pride always talked him out of it. After all, it was his father who had forced him to leave. Well, he might as well have forced him. "He left me no choice," Dreyos said to himself.

Who his friends were was none of his father's business! They were not a "bad influence" as his father so liked to point out. That incident with Old Man Karl's cattle was purely accidental. And that fight with Mayor Bale's son would never have happened if he had learned to mind his tongue.

In truth, Dreyos had grown a great deal after setting out on his own. He had learned the value of a hot meal and a warm bed, and that the work and toil spent on the farm was a small price to pay for the comforts and safety that it afforded.

The sound of a snapping twig pulled Dreyos out of his

thoughts. His hand instinctively went to the large knife on his side. Still kneeling, he slowly surveyed the area, moving his head ever so slightly.

"Probably just a squirrel," he said. His breath rose in a frosty cloud and slowly faded into the cold air.

He rose to his feet, still looking around with concern. Though he saw nothing, he felt as if he were being watched. He shivered and pulled the collar of his coat up around his ears. It did little to protect against the frigid wind. As soon as he managed to get hold of some more coin, he was going to buy some warmer clothes.

Tossing the rest of the dried beef into his mouth, he headed off north, in the direction of Lake City. Every so often, he glanced back over his shoulder to ensure that no one, or thing, was following him. He still held the knife in his hand, just in case.

Lake City, a large city with lots of taverns, would provide the opportunity to part some fools with their gold. Once he found the right crowd of people, which taverns almost always provided, he would cause a not-so-accidental accident of some sort, that he would make sure escalated into a brawl. But before it actually came to blows, he would propose a wager of a few silvers, which he usually didn't actually have, to the winner of the fight. He might even sweeten the deal by promising to use only one arm. From there, he would just let his natural talent for fighting take over. He was careful to never seriously injure anyone. A few minor cuts and bruises, sure, but that was usually the extent of it.

Dreyos wasn't proud of earning his coin by hurting people, but it didn't really bother him either. After all, he didn't force them into fighting, he just made that option a bit more difficult to avoid.

Dreyos scanned the tops of the tall, leafless trees as he made his way through the dense woods. The bitter wind howled and whistled as it passed through their skeletal limbs. This place unsettled him. He couldn't place his finger on why, but he hadn't felt comfortable since first setting foot in this forest.

Dreyos slid his leather pack around to his front and untied the flap strings. He fished around for a moment and then pulled out a rolled up piece of parchment.

He unrolled the map as he walked, checking his course. As best as he could discern, he should exit the forest at any time, then another day and a half of walking should put him in Lake City. He was so looking forward to a warm bath and sleeping on something other than the cold ground.

Dreyos rolled the map back up and replaced it in the leather pack and then did a complete turn, scanning the shadow-filled forest. The disturbing feeling of being watched had not subsided. He let out an agitated sigh and picked up his pace.

It was another hour before he finally sheathed his knife, but he remained on guard, constantly listening and looking for the slightest hint of danger. Another two hours brought the thinning edge of the forest into view.

"Finally!" he said. Just seeing the open meadow ahead lifted his spirit. It felt as if a weight had been lifted from him. He quickened his steps, eager to be out of the forest.

Dreyos was within a dozen yards from the edge of the tree line when a creature resembling a mix between a badger and a wolf leaped out from behind the dirt-filled roots of a fallen tree. A breckon. An extremely ferocious and territorial animal known for its aggressiveness.

The breckon's lips pealed back in an angry growl, revealing a mouth full of razor-sharp teeth. It shook its head from side to side, slinging thick streams of saliva to the ground. The display lasted only a moment before the creature charged, closing the distance between itself and Dreyos with impressive speed.

"Curse this forest!" Dreyos yelled as he turned and ran in the opposite direction. The breckon closed on him fast. He knew he had no chance of outrunning it, and he had no intention of trying.

Just ahead, he spotted a tall oak tree with a wide trunk; just what he was looking for. Dreyos pulled his knife from its sheath and ran straight for the tree.

The breckon was right on his heels. He could hear it

snarling and snapping. Dreyos never slowed. Just before impacting the massive oak, he leaped up and forward, one leg stretched forward leading the way. As he made contact with the tree, he pushed out hard, completely changing direction and flipping backwards over the breckon, landing safely on the ground behind it.

The breckon was caught completely off guard. It slammed hard into the base of the tree with a loud thud and a satisfying yelp, and then fell over onto its side. It was clearly addled, kicking its legs out and struggling to get back onto its feet.

Before it could right itself, Dreyos was upon it. He drove his left knee down hard into the breckon's side, pinning it to the ground with a sickly cracking sound. He slipped his knife under the breckon's neck and drew his knife deep into its flesh, releasing a crimson spray. The breckon kicked wildly for just a moment before going still.

Dreyos stood up, letting the breckon's head fall to the ground. He took a minute to catch his breath, then bent and wiped his blade clean on the beast's fur.

"Nice try," Dreyos said as he sheathed his knife. Had he not already known that breckon meat was extremely foul, no matter how you prepared it, he would have put forth the effort to skin and prepare it. Knowing better, though, he simply left it lying where it was.

He looked once more to the edge of the forest. Lake City

wasn't far now. He gave one last look at the lifeless breckon sprawled on the ground, then set out once again.

* * *

Not far into the forest from where the breckon lay, Kraelin peered out from behind a tree, watching Dreyos depart.

"Very impressive, Dreyos Harflink," Kraelin said to himself. "I do believe that you are the one I seek." A wide smile crept across his lips as he stepped out from behind the tree, setting out in the same direction Dreyos had gone.

* * *

Once clear of the forest, Dreyos breathed a lot easier. The air seemed so much lighter out on the open plain. He still couldn't quite shake the feeling of being watched though.

With night fast approaching, Dreyos scouted out a spot to make camp; a rocky overhang on the side of a small hill surrounded by several large pine trees. Using his leather pack as a pillow, he stretched out on the bare ground, one hand resting on the handle of his knife. The warmth of a fire would be most welcome, but he decided against it, preferring concealment to comfort.

Dreyos spent a long while staring out at the sky, watching the stars slowly fill the blanket of darkness above. At last, sleep found him.

With the first rays of the morning sun creeping onto the plains, Dreyos rose, anxious to be off. A breeze picked up, causing him to pull his coat tightly around his neck. He gave his shoulders a few cross-armed slaps, then set out at a brisk pace, determined to make it to Lake City before nightfall.

The land stretched out for miles ahead of him. A dusting of frost covered the ground, sparkling like diamond dust in the early morning sun. He thought of his father, who often pointed out the beauty in such things.

Not for the first time, he considered returning home, and as had become habit of late, Dreyos spoke to himself. "Why did you have to be so difficult, Father?" *I suppose I was more than a little difficult myself,* he thought. "Going home now would be admitting I was wrong. Father would never let me live that down."

Dreyos pushed the thoughts of home out of his head and concentrated on the more immediate situation; getting to Lake City and earning some coin. His first purchase would be suitable clothing and a warm meal.

That last thought made his stomach growl. He retrieved the last piece of dried beef from his pack and tossed it into his mouth. He dropped his head against a sudden gust of wind and plodded on.

The remainder of the day was relatively uneventful. The most excitement was the thunderous commotion of a grouse taking to the air. Dreyos kept up a steady pace, determined not to spend another night sleeping on the cold ground.

Just as the last rays of the evening sun were succumbing to the night's embrace, the high, stone walls of Lake City rose up in the distance.

As Dreyos drew close, he saw the two huge gates of the city entrance being pulled shut. He broke into a run, trying to reach the gates before they were completely closed. Not that they wouldn't open them again enough for him to pass through, but he would rather not have to endure the wait while they questioned him and grumbled about being inside before nightfall.

He reached the gates with just enough time to squeeze through before they slammed shut with a resonating thud.

"Hurry on with you!" one of the city guards yelled. "Are you trying to get yourself killed?"

Dreyos shot him an angry glare, but kept moving, not bothering to reply.

The city was already aglow with lanterns hanging outside of a great many of the homes and places of business. Dreyos marveled at the prosperous city sprawled before him. Merchant tents lined the streets mere feet apart. Most were packing away their goods and pulling their tents for the night, though a good many were still up, shouting out the greatness of their wares.

Dreyos paid no mind to these. He stalked past, making

his way toward a promising-looking tavern at the end of the street. It was a rugged and worn-looking place with a single lantern hanging outside the door on an ornate, but rusty, iron hook. The roaring laughter and singing from within spilled out into the street. The sign hanging near the lantern read, "The Dusty Dog".

Dreyos smiled. "My kind of place," he said, hopping over the single, broken step leading onto the porch of the establishment. He pushed the door open and headed in.

The tavern was brightly lit with several lanterns hanging upon each of the walls. A roaring fire filled a massive fireplace at one end of the common room. The Dusty Dog seemed a fitting name for the place. Most every one of its occupants looked as if they hadn't bathed in months, and the smell that hung in the air suggested no different.

Ten small tables filled the common room. Most were crowded with men and women alike, laughing and raising brimming mugs in song and toast. Dreyos spotted a small table near the center of the room that had an empty chair in front of it, along with three others that were not. He casually strolled up to the table and sat down.

"Evening," he said to the scraggly occupants of the table, giving a friendly nod and putting on a fake smile.

The three were either hard of hearing or simply didn't appreciate his company. They stared at him with blank expressions. It was just the same to Dreyos, he really didn't care how they were doing anyway.

Dreyos turned his attention back to the crowded room. A young serving maid with a tray full of frothy mugs maneuvered between tables, crossing the room in his direction. Her tight, tan shirt was cut low in the front, revealing much of her ample breasts. Her auburn hair was pulled back into a long braid that hung halfway down her back. Dreyos waved her over to the table where he sat.

"How much for a mug?" he asked, doing a poor job of keeping his eyes at the same level as hers. He gave her his best smile.

"Six coppers," she answered, seeming to take no interest in him whatsoever.

Dreyos reach inside of his coat and produced his only remaining silver coin.

"Keep the rest," he told her with a wink, tossing the coin onto the tray.

Finally smiling, the serving maid handed him a tall mug of ale. She gave him a wink and spun lightly on one heel and continued across the room. Dreyos stared intently as she walked away. Shaking his head, he lifted his mug and took a long, deep drink.

Dreyos leaned back, tilting his wooden chair onto its back legs. The three men at the table had yet to speak. He considered the biggest of the three, a gap-toothed brute at least a hundred pounds heavier than himself. He dismissed the idea quickly. Though big, he didn't look like much of a brawler.

An eruption of shouts from across the room caught his attention. A dozen men crowded around a table where two men were locked hand in hand in an arm wrestling match. Both men were of considerable size, and by the look of the match, were of near equal strengths. They struggled back and forth for a long while, and then there was a loud *snap*. A pain-filled scream split the air as the forearm of the loser broke right in the middle. His opponent mercilessly slammed the screaming man's hand onto the table.

The homely victor, a tall, wide-shouldered man with a thick head of black hair, showed no remorse for his opponent, leaping to his feet, shouting and thrusting his arms up in the air in a boastful show of victory.

Several people rushed over to the man with the broken arm and helped him out of the tavern, but most of the onlookers thronged around the winner of the match, slapping him on the back and laughing.

"No one beats Barthal!" he shouted, lifting a mug of ale to his lips and spilling as much down his front as he managed to drink.

Dreyos smiled. "Perfect."

Barthal started back toward his table, strutting like a

peacock. As he walked past, Dreyos stretched out a leg, tripping him and sending him crashing face-first into a nearby table.

"Whoa, sorry bout that, Barthole," Dreyos said, intentionally mispronouncing the man's name. Dreyos held his hands out in front of him, feigning panic as Barthal recovered and turned on him. Barthal's face was red with rage.

"I'm gonna kill you!" he screamed, clenching his fists tightly in front of him.

"Wait a minute there," Dreyos pleaded. "It was just an accident. Surely you don't expect me to fight you?"

Barthal lunged at Dreyos, taking a wild swing. Dreyos twisted his upper body and tilted to one side, cleanly dodging the man's fist without moving from where he stood.

"You *do* want me to fight you, eh!" Dreyos said, easily dodging another swing from his enraged opponent.

Dreyos held his hands out in front of him, trying to calm the man. "Since you insist on this, let's at least make it worth your while."

Barthal paused, giving Dreyos a questioning glare.

Two minutes later, Dreyos and Barthal were out on the street in front of The Dusty Dog. A mass of onlookers, all hungry to see the ensuing fight, surrounded them both.

Dreyos stood in front of Barthal, who seemed most eager to tear into this clumsy stranger who had humiliated him in front of everyone.

Dreyos held his arms out wide. "Well, how bout it then, Barthole?"

Barthal let out a battle cry and rushed Dreyos, throwing a powerful, arching swing clearly aimed for his head. Dreyos dunked under the blow and sent Barthal staggering on forward with a hard smack to the back of his head.

The crowd surged with excitement, most shouting out encouragement to their friend. "Get him Barthal! Show him who he's dealing with!"

Barthal turned back to Dreyos and slowly started toward him, grinding his teeth together and slamming a fist into his open palm. Dreyos just stood there, smiling.

When Barthal got within arm's reach, he lunged forward again, this time with a straight punch that, if it were to strike home, would undoubtedly send the best of men to the ground. But Dreyos was ready for the attack. With impressive speed and seeming ease, he turned Barthal's punch aside with an open hand and followed through by placing his other fist in the back of Barthal's head.

Barthal went down hard, falling flat on his face. He lay motionless. The crowd went silent. After a few moments, Barthal drew his arms up under him and pushed up onto his knees.

"If you're wise, you'll stay down." Dreyos hoped that he would. He was ready to collect his money and move on. Dreyos stooped down and offered Barthal his hand. Barthal proved to be the quicker this time, landing an elbow square on Dreyos' nose.

Dreyos staggered back. A warm trickle slid out of one nostril. He wiped at his nose with the back of his hand and looked down to the smear of blood. "I see," Dreyos said. His voice had now taken on a hard edge. "That, is going to cost you."

Barthal was now back on his feet and moving toward Dreyos. Dreyos closed the distance between them with a swift kick that doubled Barthal over in a gasp of pain. Dreyos slammed a knee into Barthal's face, throwing him back into an upright position. Before Barthal could react, Dreyos unleashed a blinding combination of punches into his face, the last of which sent a spray of blood onto several of the onlookers. Barthal dropped in a heap, out cold. His face was a bloody mess and one eye had already begun to swell shut.

Dreyos walked over to a toothless man who held a leather pouch in his hand.

"You have something for me?" Dreyos said.

The grungy little man swallowed hard. He never took his eyes from Barthal as he held the pouch out to Dreyos.

Dreyos snatched the pouch from the man's hand and headed back toward The Dusty dog. The crowd quietly parted before him. "Time for something to eat," he said.

Morning found Dreyos resting comfortably on a bed in the Long Potter Inn. He hastily cleaned up and headed downstairs where he was immediately greeted by the smell of fried bacon.

After cleaning his second plate, Dreyos counted his remaining coin. Just enough to buy some new clothes and pay for a couple more night's stay in the inn.

He was already planning on where he might be able to win some more coin. Word traveled fast, though, so he didn't count on being able to play the novice card again. But there were always those who would hear of his skill and feel the need to prove they were better. Dreyos welcomed them.

He stepped outside into the frigid, morning air. The streets already bustled with merchants, traders, and customers. Dreyos made his way to a large tent with wooden stands full of coats of all shapes and sizes.

"May I help you, sir?" asked the portly merchant. "I have the largest and best selection of clothing in the city. And at the best prices as well, you can be sure."

"How much for this one?" Dreyos asked, lifting a leather long coat with a thick, black lining from its peg. He proceeded to put it on while the merchant walked over to him. It fit perfectly.

"That one is twelve silvers, and a good deal at that." Without a word, Dreyos took the coat off, handed it to the merchant, and turned to leave.

"Wait," the merchant said, placing a hand on Dreyos' shoulder. "That one is on sale today. It's yours for ten silvers."

Dreyos stopped and turned to face the man, fixing him with a sobering stare. "Eight," he replied.

The man took a few moments to reply. "Ok, ok," he said. "But just don't you go telling it."

Dreyos continued down the street, wearing a new, leather long coat and carrying his old one over his shoulder. He passed by a tavern in front of which an older-looking man sat on the ground, shivering. He wore no coat, and his thin shirt was clearly not doing much to keep him warm. Dreyos dropped his old coat in the man's lap and continued without a word.

Just up the street, Dreyos spotted a familiar face. Why, if it wasn't old Barthole. And he wasn't alone. Several tall and rather stout-looking individuals accompanied him; four to be exact.

"Oh boy," Dreyos said under his breath.

Barthal and his companions made straight for him, walking with confidence, their chests puffed out. Dreyos snickered. Barthal's face was quite a mess, and one eye was still swelled shut. They stopped just a few feet in front of him.

"Good morning ladies," Dreyos said. "Why, Barthole, you look lovely this morning." Dreyos couldn't keep the sheepish grin off his face. Not that he actually tried.

"Oh you won't be so funny when we get through with you,"

Barthal said.

Dreyos noticed the short lengths of steel that two of the men produced from under their cloaks. A third brought a wooden club out from behind his back. Dreyos' smile dropped from his lips. "You're a coward Barthal. And so are your ugly sisters." Dreyos spat on Barthal's pant leg.

Barthal shook with rage. "Get him!" he yelled.

The first one to drop was Barthal, after receiving a swift kick in the face from Dreyos. Barthal's four companions rushed Dreyos.

The first of the four to close within Dreyos' reach took a fist to the nose, splaying blood across his face. He staggered back, cupping a hand over his broken nose and straining to see through tear-filled eyes.

The remaining three swarmed him, swinging their makeshift weapons with deadly intent. Dreyos dodged and ducked with fluid movement. He narrowly ducked the steel bar from the attacker directly in front of him. That one was fast.

The other two moved around to his left and right. Both lunged at him in a coordinated attack. He spun past one of the men, easily avoiding the clumsy thrust of his steel bar. He thought he had put himself out of the reach of the other man, but underestimated his reach. A bright flash filled his vision as a wooden club crashed into the back of his head, dropping him to his knees.

Dreyos' vision blurred, but he managed to shake it off. He hooked the ankle of one of the thugs with his foot, sweeping his leg out from under him and dropping him flat on his back. Dreyos rolled to his left, just missing the end of a steel bar as it smashed into the ground where his head had just been. As he rolled onto his back, Dreyos slammed his elbow into the throat of the fallen man. The ruffian made a loud, gurgling sound. A high-pitched, whistling sound escaped his lips as he grasped at his throat, struggling to draw in air.

Dreyos flipped back up to his feet, barely dodging a blur of steel before crushing the knee of his attacker with a well-placed kick. The man's knee bent backward with a snap. He collapsed to the ground, clutching his destroyed knee and screaming in agony.

Dreyos whirled around just in time to grab the arm of the man wielding the club, stopping it in mid-swing. Dreyos head bunted him squared in the face and drew his free arm back for a punch, but something struck him in the side of the chest, driving the wind out of him. Dreyos was certain he heard his ribs crack.

Before Dreyos could recover, something solid smashed into his face, and another heavy blow landed hard into his left shoulder. He fell to the ground. His ears were ringing, and everything was spinning.

A powerful kick to his side rolled him onto his back. Barthal stood over him, holding a bar of steel with both hands. "You're not laughing now, are you?" Barthal said, raising the bar up above his head.

A hand suddenly appeared over Barthal's shoulder and wrenched the bar out of his hands. Barthal spun around to see who dared interfere and was met by a fist to his chest that knocked him completely off his feet. He landed square on his shoulders several feet away.

The two men that were still able to fight rushed forward to take care of the newcomer, but as they realized that this new fighter was an old man, they paused in confusion; a hesitation that cost them dearly.

In the split second it took to widen their eyes in surprise, the old man sent all of them sprawling to the ground with an unnaturally fast combination of open-handed strikes.

Dreyos groaned in pain as he forced himself up onto one knee. His head pounded, and every breath caused him to wince. All his attackers were moaning and struggling to their feet, those with lesser injuries helping the others. They all staggered or limped away without another word.

The old man had a hooded cloak pulled around him. It was covered in green and brown patterns resembling leaves. He walked over to Dreyos and offered him a hand. Dreyos gratefully accepted. He couldn't hold back a grunt of pain as he allowed the stranger to help pull him up to his feet. His entire right arm was numb. He held it against his injured side with

his good hand.

"Thank you," Dreyos said.

"Think nothing of it," the old man said. Dreyos got his first good look at his rescuer. His face was full of wrinkles and his back bent with age.

"How did you do that?" Dreyos said. "I mean," Dreyos paused, looking for the right way to put it.

"Yes, I know. I'm an old man. And you are a stubborn young man who has much to learn. Assuming you are willing to learn, that is."

"Who are you, and what makes you think that you know anything about me?" Dreyos said. He stared at the old man with a mix of thankfulness and confusion.

"My name is Kraelin Dregthorn. Come with me, Dreyos Harflink, and I will explain." Kraelin turned and walked away, heading in the direction of the city gates.

"Wait just a minute! How do you know my name? Where are you going?"

"Follow me, and you shall know," the old man said without pausing.

Dreyos stared after him, shaking his head. It was apparent the old man didn't intend to stop. With a sigh, he set out after him, clutching his injured side and groaning with each step.

Together, they left Lake City, heading for the nearby hills.

Dreyos had no idea of where they were going. For close to an hour they walked in silence. Dreyos thought several times to insist on knowing where they were headed and what the old man was about, but in the end he decided to remain silent.

Finally, the old man spoke. "So I see that you can actually control that tongue of yours."

Dreyos felt his temper rising until the old man turned and gave him a warm smile. Dreyos chuckled. "Yeah. I guess I can," he said.

"I can teach you to control much more than that, if you wish."

Dreyos had no idea what the old man was talking about, and hadn't completely ruled out the possibility that he was a bit touched. But what did he have to lose?

"I'm all ears," Dreyos said.

The old man stopped and turned, looking Dreyos in the eyes. "Good," he said. "I have much to share with you. But it can wait till tomorrow." Without another word, he turned and resumed walking.

That was fine with Dreyos. Right now, he just wanted to lie down. His head was still pounding, and each breath sent stabs of pain through his chest.

It was another hour before the trees at last gave way to a clearing that revealed a small hut built from saplings and elephant leaves. The green limbs and freshly trampled weeds gave the distinct impression that the place was only recently constructed.

The inside of the hut was as simple as the outside. A layer of blankets lay spread out in the middle of the floor. A large, leather backpack lay on the floor next to them. Other than that, the place was empty.

After removing a few of the blankets and spreading them out near the others, Kraelin motioned toward them. "Get some rest, Dreyos. We have much to discuss in the morning."

Without waiting for Dreyos to settle in, he walked back outside, speaking as he went. "I have some things to tend to. I will be back soon."

It was still early in the day, but Dreyos was exhausted. Despite the pain, he managed to fall asleep shortly after laying down.

Dreyos woke to a strong herbal scent that made him wrinkle his nose. He sat up, wincing at the pain in his side. Kraelin sat cross-legged next to him, sipping from a steaming cup. "I have one for you too," he said, picking up another cup. He held it out to Dreyos.

"It will help with the soreness and speed your recovery. Myself, I just enjoy the taste."

Dreyos accepted the cup. A steady flow of steam rose from its contents, fading into the cold air. He hesitantly took a sip. It was an exceptionally sweet tea that, to Kraelin's credit, tasted much better than it smelled.

As Dreyos drained the last of the tea from the cup, Kraelin stood and motioned toward the door. "Let's take a walk," he said.

They stepped out into the crisp, morning air. The sun had just broken over the horizon. Dreyos was shocked that he had slept so long.

Kraelin stood for a long moment with his head tilted back, breathing deeply. A satisfied smile crept onto his face. It was obvious the old man enjoyed the outdoors.

"You have an exceptional gift, Dreyos," he said, lowering his head and fixing Dreyos with a serious look. "You have managed to tap into it to a small degree without even knowing it."

The old man paused, looking at Dreyos. "I, too, have this gift. I have been aware of you for some time now, Dreyos. You have great potential, and I believe you to be a worthy student."

Dreyos found it quite intriguing, to be sure, but had serious doubts as to where this was leading. He held his tongue though, for now.

"Our spirits are a great deal stronger than that of the average man. But most importantly, we can control our spirits. And this, Dreyos, makes us quite different than most."

"So you're telling me that you are some kind of super-being, and that I am too?" Dreyos said, not making an effort to hide the doubt in his words.

"Yes. I suppose that is as good a summary as any. Simply put, the spirit controls the body, and if you control the spirit, then you also control the body."

Dreyos raised an eyebrow at Kraelin's matter-of-fact response. "Control the body?" Dreyos said. "I didn't realize that I wasn't in control of my body."

Kraelin shot Dreyos an angry glare. "Allow me to demonstrate," he said. He drew a dagger from the inside of his coat and offered it to Dreyos. "Take it," he said. His voice was calm but commanding.

Dreyos took the dagger as instructed. The double-edged blade dropped to a needle-fine point.

"Now strike me," Kraelin said.

"You're mad. I don't want to kill you, old man."

Kraelin struck out with incredible speed, slapping Dreyos hard in the face.

"You will refer to me as Kraelin, nothing other. Now do as I say."

Dreyos' eyes narrowed in anger. "Why do you want me to kill you?" he said, gritting his teeth.

"You flatter yourself," Kraelin said. "Now do as I say," Kraelin said, his voice taking on an angry tone.

Maybe the old man was mad after all. Dreyos thought back to the fight outside The Dusty Dog. The old man had moved with surprising speed, and showed skill and strength that didn't seem possible for one of his age.

Dreyos decided to humor him, trusting that the old man was more than capable of dodging his attack. He thrust the dagger forward.

Kraelin didn't move at all. Dreyos' eyes went wide with shock when the dagger sunk deep into Kraelin's stomach. Kraelin didn't even flinch. He just smiled.

Dreyos immediately pulled the dagger back and dropped it to the ground. He grabbed hold of Kraelin to steady him, expecting him to collapse at any moment.

"I'm fine," Kraelin said. "You didn't hurt me."

Dreyos stared in disbelief. There should have been a gushing wound in Kraelin's stomach, but there was no blood at all, only a clean slice in Kraelin's coat where the dagger had sliced through.

"I don't understand. You really aren't hurt," Dreyos said, spreading open the slice in Kraelin's shirt. There wasn't even a mark. Had he not witnessed this firsthand, he wouldn't have believed it.

"As I told you, the spirit controls the body. Your attack was with your body alone. It was no threat to one who has full control of their spirit."

Dreyos now hung on Kraelin's every word.

"The pain you feel now, from your recent injuries, is not necessary. Only your body has been harmed. Had you control over your spirit, you could avoid such discomforts," Kraelin said.

"Teach me how," Dreyos pleaded.

"I will. But you are not yet ready. There are things you must first learn, and things you must forget. My time is short, and I hope to pass my knowledge on to you before I move on, but this will not be easy, and it will not be quick. It could take years to master these abilities."

"I'm a quick learner," Dreyos said. "When can we start?"

"Soon. But we must leave this place first. I have a home in the near mountains. There is where I will teach you."

"Great!" Dreyos said, not bothering to hide the excitement in his voice.

A few minutes later, the two of them set out for the Krag Mountains.

The passing of the next several months felt like only a few weeks to Dreyos. He eagerly soaked in Kraelin's lessons, giving himself fully to them. His respect for Kraelin grew with each passing day. The man was exceptionally wise, and selfless. He dedicated nearly every waking moment to teaching Dreyos, and had taught him much more than utilizing his gift to control his spirit.

The training was not at all what Dreyos expected. What he thought would be a seizing of some hidden power turned out to be much more akin to coaxing a feeble ember to life. It often required seeking an inner calm and embracing the harsh truths of self-reflection. Kraelin's instruction was far removed from the style of training that Dreyos was used to.

Dreyos crested the final slope to the flat where Kraelin's cabin sat. He adjusted the large pack of supplies he carried on his back and picked up the pace. The hike up from Windrum, a small village near the mountain's base, took the better part of three hours.

Dreyos had gotten accustomed to the regular trip, and even enjoyed it. He smiled when he noticed Kraelin sitting in his favorite spot in front of the cabin, sipping from a small cup.

After putting the supplies away, Dreyos joined Kraelin outside, pulling up a chair beside him.

Kraelin stared out at the blue sky. A lone hawk circled in the distance. It was a beautiful day.

"Dreyos," Kraelin said, still staring ahead.

"Yes," Dreyos said.

"You remember, when first we met, that I told you that my time was short?"

Dreyos remembered, but didn't like to think about the implications, and had never brought it back up. "I do," Dreyos said, doing a poor job of masking the uneasiness in his voice.

"I grow weaker each day. I have lived a long and fruitful life, but my time is coming very soon. I am proud of you, Dreyos.

You have grown greatly in our short time together."

"Thank you, Kraelin," Dreyos said. "Is everything alright?"

Kraelin slowly stood up. "I just need to rest." His voice sounded so weak.

Dreyos put an arm around him and walked him to his bedroom. After helping Kraelin into bed, Dreyos poured a glass of water from a pitcher and set it on the small, bedside table.

"I'll leave you to it then," Dreyos said with a smile, trying to sound as lighthearted as possible. "If you need anything, give me a shout. I'll be just outside."

Kraelin reached out and patted the back of Dreyos' hand.

Once outside, Dreyos stood in silence. A tear ran down his cheek. *I have been so stubborn and missed out on so much.* As he had done often of late, he thought of his parents. His tears now came heavily.

Kraelin grew steadily weaker over the next few days, and Dreyos was there, patiently tending to all of his needs.

Dreyos knelt beside of Kraelin's bed, wiping his head with a damp cloth. "I have to go to Windrum for some lamp oil. I didn't realize we were so low or I would have picked some up on my last trip. I will hurry. Will you be ok until I return?"

"I will be fine," Kraelin said. The strain in his voice didn't sound convincing at all.

Dreyos strapped his knife to his side, threw a leather pack

over one shoulder, and headed down the mountain. He was nearly to the bottom when he leaped from one small ledge to another, instead of taking the longer way around and down.

As he landed, the ledge broke away. Dreyos plummeted down the steep slope, tumbling and rolling with several large rocks close behind. As he slid to a stop, a shower of dirt and rocks slammed into him before he could get out of the way.

A jagged boulder, nearly as big as he was, caught him on the side of the face. He felt the flesh rip free as the force of the blow staggered him back. Dreyos instinctively fell back into his training and the wound disappeared as fast as it was inflicted.

Dreyos took a moment to dust himself off. He had a few tears in his shirt, but there wasn't a scratch or bruise on him. Shaking the last bit of dirt out of his hair, he set off once more.

Once in the village, Dreyos headed straight for the general merchant store. Normally, he would spend a few minutes visiting with some of the friends he had made here in Windrum, but there was no time for such pleasantries today.

Dreyos pulled Kraelin's leather coin pouch from his pocket as he entered Thad's store. Kraelin had made a fine living over the years by selling the rare herbs he gathered from high in the Krag Mountains. Dreyos wasted no time purchasing several flasks of oil and some more of Kraelin's favorite tea.

Dreyos had just left the store when he heard a man's voice pleading for mercy behind a nearby house. He quickly rounded the house and saw one of his friends, Lynden, curled up on the ground, doing his best to protect himself against the brutal kicks of the wide-shouldered man standing over him. A saddled horse stood nearby, grazing upon a cabbage in Lynden's garden.

Dreyos yelled at the man. "If I were you, I would stop right there!"

The man paused, turning to look at Dreyos. "Is that right? Well, if I were you, I would mind my own business," the man said. He was a full hand taller than Dreyos and wore a tight-fitting shirt clearly intended to show off his muscular chest.

Dreyos felt his temper rising, but pushed it down, forcing himself to be calm.

"What right have you to assault this man?" Dreyos asked, hoping to find out what this was about and perhaps avoid further trouble.

"He accused me of stealing from his pitiful little garden," the man replied.

"I merely asked you not to ride your horse through it, when you-" Lynden was cut off in mid-sentence as the stranger slammed a boot into his gut.

"Oh, do shut up!" the man yelled at Lynden.

Dreyos' control of his calm shattered. He sat his leather pack on the ground and stalked toward the arrogant intruder.

"How about trying that with me?" Dreyos said, spreading

his arms out in invitation.

"Well, aren't we the brave one?" the man said, laughing. "I think you need to show me a little more respect, boy. I would hate to have to hurt you."

Dreyos stopped just a few feet away from the mouthy man, locking eyes with him.

"Ever hear the name Drosdane before, boy?" the man said.

"Can't say that I have," Dreyos said. He noted the man's clothing. His shirt was black silk. His pants and leather boots were a matching black. All of this man's apparel looked very expensive. His hair and face, though, didn't match his clothes. His dark brown hair spilled onto his shoulders in a matted mess, and his short beard looked as though it had been trimmed with a dull knife.

"Well now you have," the man said. He lunged forward with a punch aimed for Dreyos' nose. Dreyos reflexively dodged to the side and grabbed Drosdane's arm, twisting it behind his back and shoving him toward the wall of the house. As Drosdane staggered forward, he kicked backwards with explosive speed, connecting solidly in Dreyos' stomach.

Dreyos staggered back, releasing the hold on Drosdane's arm. The kick was hard, and solid. Dreyos struggled to regain his breath. He hadn't had more than a second to do so before Drosdane turned and was upon him.

Drosdane came in hard with a blinding combination of

punches and kicks. Dreyos was pressed into a solely defensive role but somehow managed to avoid or block every strike that Drosdane threw.

Fists and hands intertwined in a dizzying flurry, each seeking the opening that would allow a clean hit. Dreyos finally managed to take the offensive, backing Drosdane up several steps with a solid strike to the chest. This man was, by far, the most skilled opponent he had ever faced.

Drosdane stared at Dreyos, a noticeable look of confusion upon his face. "You're good."

Dreyos made no reply. If a look of confusion was not on his own face, then he did a good job of hiding it. That kick to his stomach had been quite painful, and still, his breath didn't come as easy as it should. Dreyos tried to clear his mind and focus on what he had learned from Kraelin. He was just taken by surprise, that's all.

"Get on your horse and leave, while you're still able," Dreyos said.

"Not so quick, boy. I'm not through with you yet!" Drosdane came in again, this time with a spinning kick. Dreyos batted it aside and retaliated with a kick of his own. Drosdane ducked it with seeming ease, coming up with a speeding back fist.

Dreyos threw both forearms up, blocking the attack. The force of the blow was tremendous. A jolt of pain shot up his arms from the point of impact. He staggered back a step, his arms throbbing. How was it that he couldn't overcome the pain?

Drosdane threw a straight punch, missing Dreyos' head by less than an inch. Dreyos countered instantly, feigning a punch but then coming up and across with an elbow. The tip of Dreyos' elbow caught Drosdane just over his left eye, instantly opening his skin. Blood streamed from the wide gash and trickled down the inside of Drosdane's nose.

Drosdane stepped back and pressed a palm to his forehead. Dreyos stood silently, ready for Drosdane to make his next move.

Drosdane pulled his hand down and stared at the blood covering his hand. He looked back up at Dreyos, a wild look in his eyes. He seemed genuinely shocked to see his own blood. In a flash, Drosdane produced a slim dagger from one of his boots and leaped toward Dreyos.

Dreyos was ready, twisting to one side and cleanly avoiding the dagger. Drosdane attacked with ferocity, using the dagger to lead the way for his punches and kicks. Dreyos dodged and blocked methodically, foiling Drosdane's every attack, but he couldn't manage to find an opening to draw his own blade and even the odds.

Dreyos had thus far managed to hold his own, but the talent and speed of his opponent's attacks left no room for error. Dreyos started for his knife but realized he didn't have time and aborted the effort. Unfortunately, his hesitation gave Drosdane the opening he needed. Drosdane's dagger slipped through his defenses, cutting cleanly through his shirt and drawing a line of blood across his stomach.

Dreyos reflexively dropped a hand to his injured stomach, further opening his defenses. Drosdane capitalized on the opportunity, landing a kick to Dreyos' chest that sent him to the ground.

Dreyos took advantage of the fall, rolling away from Drosdane and coming back up with his knife in his hand. Drosdane was already moving toward him but stopped when he realized that Dreyos was now armed.

They both stared at one another for a long moment, neither saying a word.

Dreyos broke the silence with a yell and charged at Drosdane; his knife raised high. Dreyos had no intention of actually trying to follow through with such an amateur maneuver, but he hoped that Drosdane thought that he would, even if only for an instant.

As he closed the gap to Drosdane, Dreyos suddenly dropped to one knee, spinning away and driving his knife backwards and up. Drosdane was caught off guard by the maneuver and wasn't able to avoid the strike. Dreyos' blade sunk deep into the inside of Drosdane's right leg. Dreyos pulled the knife free as he continued his spin, coming back around to face Drosdane.

Drosdane dropped to the ground, clutching at his leg and wailing in agony. Blood spurted from the wound. Drosdane crawled backwards toward his horse. Dreyos didn't pursue him but stood in silence as Drosdane made his way to his horse and pulled himself up into the saddle.

"Don't ever come back," Dreyos said between deep breaths.

"I don't know who you are, but I do know *what* you are! And I *will* be back! You can count on that." Drosdane turned his horse and raced off into the distance and out of sight.

Dreyos turned his attention to Lynden, who was now on his feet, leaning against the side of his house.

"Are you alright?" Dreyos said, rushing over to his friend. "I'm fine," Lynden said. "I should be the one asking you that."

"I'll be ok," Dreyos said, still struggling to catch his breath. "Do you know that, man?" Dreyos asked.

Lynden shook his head no. "Never seen him before."

"Let's hope neither of us does again," Dreyos said. "Take care, friend. I have to get back to Kraelin."

"Thank you, Dreyos," Lynden said.

Dreyos scooped up his leather pack and set off. His shirt was covered in blood. The cut didn't look deep, but it was certainly painful.

What had just happened? The pain, this cut, Drosdane's

words to him before riding off. Dreyos had a terrible feeling about this encounter.

Several hours later, Dreyos walked quietly into Kraelin's room and kneeled beside of his bed.

Kraelin was asleep. Dreyos gently placed a hand on his mentor's shoulder. Kraelin jumped slightly at the touch, then turned to face Dreyos. "You are back," Kraelin said.

"Yes," Dreyos said. "I had some-- problems, while in Windrum."

"Problems?" Kraelin said.

"How many others, like us, do you think exist?" Dreyos said.

Kraelin's eyes narrowed on Dreyos, taking on a sharp edge. "Very few, I would guess. Besides you, I have never actually met another, other than my teacher who died many years ago. Why do you ask?"

Dreyos stood and raised his shirt to reveal his blood-caked abdomen. The wound had finally stopped bleeding, but it was obvious that it would need to be stitched up.

"Who did this to you?" Kraelin said as he pushed himself up onto one elbow. His voice was louder now and full of concern.

"He calls himself Drosdane," Dreyos said. "He's like us, isn't he?"

"If he did this to you, then he must be," Kraelin said.

Dreyos swallowed hard, thinking of the seriousness of the situation. This man had the ability to destroy both body and soul. "He could have killed me," Dreyos spoke to himself as much as to Kraelin.

Kraelin swung his feet onto the floor. "Let's tend to that wound," he said. "In the morning, I will teach you your final lesson."

Dreyos and Kraelin were already outside as the sun broke over the horizon. Kraelin sat in his usual chair, and Dreyos stood facing him. Kraelin's eyes looked so tired, and his breathing was slow and raspy. It pained Dreyos to see him like this. His health had declined so fast.

"I have taught you many things, young Dreyos, and in the years to come, you will learn much more. With the knowledge I have given you, and the gift you possess, you will live many years longer than you would have otherwise. But when your time comes, as mine has, it will come quickly."

It pained Dreyos to hear such words, but he listened respectfully.

"As I have, you too will feel the need to pass on your knowledge. When your days begin to slow, look for another with this gift and teach him as I have you. It may be that you won't find anyone, but you must try. It's very important that this knowledge not be lost. And perhaps more important is that it doesn't come into the hands of the wrong type of man."

"Men like Drosdane," Dreyos said.

"Yes. Men like him," Kraelin said. "I wish peace for you,

Dreyos, but Drosdane must be dealt with. He will cause much suffering and destruction for many years if not stopped."

Dreyos nodded his agreement.

"I have one last thing to teach you. A secret passed on to me by my teacher. It is a powerful technique, but it must be used with the greatest of caution. If used carelessly, it will kill you."

The next two hours were spent with Kraelin talking and Dreyos listening. Demonstrating the process for focusing one's spirit into a surge was a difficult and draining process. Dreyos tried several times to get Kraelin to rest, but he insisted on finishing the lesson. Learning of Drosdane, such an obviously cruel and destructive man with the ability to control his spirit, had visibly shaken Kraelin.

Dreyos gave Kraelin his full attention and best effort, but he wasn't able to create the spirit surge that Kraelin demonstrated.

"I'm sorry, Kraelin. I promise I will keep practicing until I get it, but will you please rest now?"

"You have nothing to be sorry for, Dreyos. I didn't expect you to succeed right away. It will come." His voice quivered as he spoke.

Kraelin placed a hand on Dreyos' shoulder and looked him in the eye. "Live your life with no regrets. You have a good heart. Listen to it." He pulled Dreyos into a hug and whispered in his ear. "My time has come. Good-bye, Dreyos." Kraelin exhaled deeply, then went limp.

Dreyos grabbed hold of Kraelin before he could fall to the ground. He scooped him into his arms and carried him inside to his bead, laying him down gently.

Tears filled Dreyos' eyes. He fell to his knees, trembling. He stared at Kraelin in silence for a few moments then threw his head back, releasing a long, bitter wail. This hurt was far worse than anything he had suffered at the hands of any of his opponents.

After several hours of mourning, Dreyos carefully lifted Kraelin out of his bed and carried him to a small field not far from the cabin. There, he buried his mentor and friend.

Dreyos couldn't stand to stay in Kraelin's cabin. The memories it stirred were too painful. Instead, he spent the next several weeks in Windrum as Lynden's guest. He kept himself busy by helping Lynden with his garden and other daily chores. He also spent several hours each evening practicing the techniques Kraelin had taught him, especially the final lesson that still eluded him.

Dreyos wasn't sure how long he planned to stay in Windrum, but he just couldn't bring himself to go yet. He had unfinished business here and felt it was only a matter of time before that business showed itself again.

Late one evening, one month to the day after Kraelin's passing, Dreyos walked along a dirt road on the outskirt of

Windrum carrying a stringer of fish caught from the nearby river. He suddenly had the overwhelming feeling that he was not alone. His skin tingled, and goose bumps ran down both arms in a chilling wave.

Dreyos spun around to see Drosdane standing not more than a dozen paces behind him, feet spread apart and holding a dagger in one hand.

"How's your stomach?" Drosdane said. His lips parted in an arrogant sneer.

"Fine," Dreyos said. "How's the leg?"

"It's healed well enough," Drosdane said, his smile now gone.

Drosdane started toward Dreyos at a fast walk. "You should know, I don't intend to leave you alive."

"That's interesting. I was thinking the same thing about you," Dreyos said, dropping the stringer of fish and his fishing pole. He drew his knife from his belt and charged.

As the two met, Drosdane leaped forward with a dagger thrust. Dreyos twisted out of the way and countered with a crosscut of his own blade, but Drosdane deftly bobbed out of reach.

Both came at each other hard and fast, blades ringing out loudly as they repeatedly clashed together and slid apart. Bodies swirled around each other, kicking and punching, slashing and dodging. Neither managed a successful strike against the other, but their intensity never lessened. Dreyos fought with a single goal in mind; Drosdane must die.

Time and time again, a blade or fist came dangerously close to connecting, but was always dodged or deflected at the last possible moment.

Unbelievably, Drosdane managed to pick up the intensity, unleashing an astonishing series of punches and thrusts that sent Dreyos reeling backwards. Drosdane maintained perfect form and moved with astonishing speed. At last, he managed to slip his dagger through Dreyos' guard, drawing a line of blood across Dreyos' left cheek.

Drosdane had overextended slightly with that last move, though, and Dreyos grabbed his wrist. He twisted Drosdane's arm to the outside, trying to force the dagger out of his hand while simultaneously thrusting his own knife toward Drosdane's stomach.

Drosdane managed to grab Dreyos' wrist before the blade could find its mark. He pulled in close to Dreyos. There they stood, locked together, staring into each other's eyes.

"It doesn't have to be like this," Drosdane said. "We could work together. With our combined abilities, there's nothing we could not accomplish, nothing we could not have."

"I would rather die," Dreyos said, pushing Drosdane backwards, breaking their holds on one another.

"So be it," Drosdane said. His right leg came up and around

with a kick aimed for Dreyos' head. Dreyos spun in and past Drosdane's leg, completing a full turn that ended with a powerful kick of his own that caught Drosdane full in the chest, sending him to the ground.

Dreyos moved in on him quickly, not wanting to give him a chance to recover. As he dropped low, coming down with his knife, Drosdane kicked out, catching Dreyos in the stomach. He pushed up and backwards, sending Dreyos flipping over and behind him. Dreyos landed flat on his back.

Though slightly winded, it wasn't nearly enough to stop Dreyos. He rolled over and sprang back up to his feet. Unfortunately, this also gave Drosdane time to get up.

Dreyos immediately took the offensive, lunging forward with his knife. Drosdane jumped back, narrowly escaping the strike. He answered by feigning a low kick and simultaneously slinging a handful of dirt into Dreyos' face.

Dreyos staggered backward, trying to force his eyes into focus. Drosdane snapped his arm forward, releasing his dagger. It sunk deep into Dreyos' left shoulder.

Dreyos yelled out in pain and grabbed the handle of the dagger. He saw the blurry form of Drosdane charging at him, but didn't react in time. Drosdane plowed into him, knocking him to the ground, following to land on top of him. The force of the landing sent Dreyos' knife flying out of his hand. It landed several feet out of reach.

Drosdane didn't give Dreyos a chance to retaliate. He grabbed both of Dreyos' wrists and head bunted him in the face. Dreyos felt his nose break. The pain was intense.

Dreyos tried to roll out from under Drosdane, but Drosdane managed to keep him down. With a quick twist, Dreyos slipped his right arm free and slammed a fist into the side of Drosdane's head. Drosdane seemed unfazed.

Dreyos' eyes continued to water. He was struggling to see anything at all now. Drosdane grabbed his right wrist and pinned it to the ground again.

Dreyos fought to pull his left arm free as well, but it had no strength. The dagger, still sticking in his shoulder, must have done some serious damage. He could feel his blood streaming from the wound.

Drosdane suddenly let go of Dreyos' left arm and slammed his forearm into Dreyos' throat. He pressed down hard, leaning his weight forward.

Dreyos gagged, unable to draw in a breath. A shroud of blackness closed in on him. The image of Kraelin's grave came to him. Was he going to join Kraelin in the blackness of death?

His final lesson with Kraelin came to him. He called on the last of his strength, falling into the technique that he had so far failed to master.

Dreyos exerted his control over his spirit, shifting it and

drawing it together. His spirit flowed into his right hand, gathering and concentrating. Dreyos felt the darkness pressing in around him; if this failed, he would die.

Dreyos' hand began to burn with a powerful energy. He clenched his hand into a tight fist then struck out with all of his remaining strength. There was a bright flash at the moment Dreyos' fist slammed into Drosdane's head. The built up energy shot into Drosdane. There was a tremendous pop as his head exploded under the might of the blow. His body fell limp to the ground.

Dreyos gasped deeply, filling his burning lungs with air. He rolled over and pushed up onto his knees, rubbing his neck. His head pounded and his shoulder throbbed. He grasped the handle of Drosdane's dagger and pulled, screaming in pain as the blade slid free.

Dreyos fell onto his back, thoroughly exhausted. He lay there for several minutes, staring into the sky.

* * *

The sun was just beginning to rise as Graylin came out of the house and headed toward the barn. He paused when a distant noise caught his attention. Was that someone yelling? He turned, straining to see who it might be.

Just coming into sight, across the large, open field that bordered the farm, he could make out someone running and

waving their arms.

"Could it be?" Graylin said, his voice cracked and tears immediately began welling up in his eyes. "Could it really be?"

Dreyos came running into sight and leaped the short fence bordering the field. He ran right up to Graylin before stopping.

They stood in silence for a moment staring at one another, and then Dreyos threw his arms around his father, lifting him off the ground and squeezing him in a tight hug.

They held onto each other for a long while, tears of joy streaming down their faces.

Dreyos had a lot to make up for, and he was more than ready to begin.

The Tormented

ZACH WALLEN SAT AT A CROWDED TABLE in the cafeteria of Karson Wells Penitentiary, staring at his tray. Mashed potatoes, peas, and a round piece of meat covered in brown, jelly-like gravy sat untouched. The air hung thick with the buzz of conversation and the clang of plastic food trays.

Hardly aware of the conversation at his table, Zack's thoughts were filled with visions of death and violence. Last night, as with most nights, Zack's sleep had been haunted by a morbid replaying of the incident that had landed him in prison.

To those in the bar, it seemed clear that Zack had killed the man, but of course they could not see the ever-present tormentor and self-appointed protector that always shadowed Zack and could, and often did, take control of his body.

Zack let out a heavy sigh, pressing his palm over his eyes and resting his fingers on his freshly shaved scalp. Slowly withdrawing from his dismal thoughts, Zack turned his attention to the loud inmate who seemed to have the attention of everyone at the table.

"They put Dawson in the Mad Room yesterday," the man sitting directly across from Zack said. He leaned forward on his elbows, slowly eyeing the others at the table and pausing for effect. Brown gravy hung from his chin, but he paid it no attention. "I didn't know a man could scream like that. What ya bet he's dead when they go to let him out?"

Several men at the table murmured their agreement. Zack stared at the man with gravy on his chin, his interest suddenly caught. "What's this, *Mad Room?*" Zack asked.

"Solitary," answered a heavy inmate sitting to Zack's left. "And the last place you ever wanna be."

A gangly-looking inmate with several missing teeth and deep-set eyes took the opportunity to jump into the conversation and educate this newcomer; Zack had only been transferred to Karson Wells three days prior.

"Depends on who you ask, I suppose. Some say it's a result of some kind of magnetic energy coming up from the ground. Some say it's just the result of solitary confinement. But the truth is, that room is haunted." The man shivered. "Whatever the cause, it's called the Mad Room cause don't no one come out of there the same."

Haunted. Wouldn't that be something? Zack looked to his left, taking notice of the wide-shouldered guard standing near the doorway to the cafeteria. "I hope you're right," he said, as much to himself as to those at his table.

Zack picked up his tray as he stood and started across the cafeteria, his pulse growing with each step. "This prison is a joke," he said loudly enough to draw everyone's attention. "And the guards are a bunch of sissies," he said, using the most arrogant tone he could manage. He veered away from the tray deposit and made as if he was going to walk past the guard and out of the cafeteria.

The guard, who was at least a foot taller than Zack, with a thick, square jaw that gave him the appearance of a pit bull, stepped in front of Zack. "Your tray goes over there, loud mouth," the guard said as he unfolded his arms and pointed to his right.

"I didn't ask," Zack said, staring defiantly into the guard's eyes. Zack let his tray of food drop. It hit the floor with a loud smack, spraying mashed potatoes and gravy all over the legs of the guard's neatly pressed pants. The cafeteria went deathly quiet as all eyes went to Zack and the guard.

The guard drew out the slender black club hanging from his belt and pushed at Zack's chest with the tip. "You're gonna wish you hadn't done that," he said.

Zack felt the presence of his demonic companion stirring, its fury building. "Yeah, right," Zack said with a smirk. Then he spit in the officer's face.

The officer drew back his club, and Zack shuddered with a wave of cold fury as the demon entered him. Zack moved with unnatural speed, ducking under the swinging club and grabbing the officer between the legs with one hand and by the front of his shirt with the other. As Zack straightened, he lifted the officer over his head and launched him several feet through the air, landing him flat on his back in the middle of a nearby table. It cracked and buckled under the impact, but held together.

The guard rolled from the table with a groan, quickly getting back on his feet. He slapped the club into an open hand and stalked toward Zack. Two other guards came charging in from either side of the room.

Zack bit down hard on his tongue. The metallic taste of blood bloomed in his mouth. His eyes blurred with tears from the pain, but the distraction worked. The demon's fury shifted from the guards and turned on Zack himself. A deep growl rumbled in the back of Zack's throat. His body went rigid, and his vision darkened as the demon attempted to subdue him.

Zack struggled to remain conscious and continuing biting down on his tongue as the guards threw him to the floor, forcing his arms behind his back and handcuffing him.

A few minutes later, Zack stood just inside the entrance of the mad room, his wrists still handcuffed behind his back. The large guard Zack had assaulted, stood in front of him once again. "We'll see how tough you are after a few days in solitary. I think you'll find that Karson Wells is anything but a joke."

Zack smiled as the heavy steel door slammed in his face, plunging him into complete darkness.

The smell of sweat, mold, and the acrid stench of urine permeated the cramped room. Zack spent what felt like several hours pacing in circles, listening and waiting. Then, at last, it began.

The sudden feeling that someone was watching him caused the hair on his neck to stand on end. A chill raced over his skin as the familiar fury of his demonic protector surrounded him. The demon sensed a threat to Zack. Something was in the room.

A low growl rose within the darkness. Zack shuddered as the demon plunged inside of him, taking control. In that instant, Zack was able to see through the demon's eyes. A hideous figure floated inches from his face. Its naked body looked much like that of a bloated, rotten corpse. The eyes of the floating figure were great black orbs the size of pool balls.

Its over-sized mouth opened wide, revealing dozens of long, needle-sharp teeth. They dripped with thick saliva.

Zack reflexively jumped back, slamming into the cold, concrete wall. Though he had hoped for the presence of another demon, he couldn't control his terror at the site of the thing. His scream reverberated inside the tiny room.

Zack's knees gave out as his demon lunged out of his body, colliding with the intruder. The mad room shook with inhuman wails and shrieks as the two entities fought. The maddening sounds reverberated with ear-shattering intensity. The supernatural cacophony continued for several minutes before all suddenly fell silent.

* * *

It was late the next morning before the guards opened the door to the mad room. The heavy door slowly swung open, revealing two guards standing nervously to either side and a third guard standing directly ahead.

Zack stood in the doorway with his head down. His arms hung by his sides. He still wore handcuffs on his wrists, but the connecting chain had been snapped in two. His head slowly rose.

Without a word, Zack stepped out of the room, and his two supernatural companions exited with him. The guards on either side stepped forward, reaching for his arms.

Zack welcomed the demon and it instantly seized control. The air exploded with a deafening shriek from an unseen entity. Zack struck both guards in the chest with his palms, shattering ribs and sending them sprawling to the floor.

The third guard drew his pistol, but Zack, or more appropriately, the demon, was too quick. With one hand, he lifted the guard off the floor by his throat and simultaneously relieved him of his pistol with the other.

In a matter of seconds, four more guards rushed into the corridor. Each of them had pistols drawn and trained on Zack. "Drop the gun and let him go," one of the guards yelled.

Zack no longer cared whether he lived or died. His relentless torment had just doubled, and these guards now presented him with a means to an end. He had no desire to kill any of them--but they didn't know that. With a roar, Zack slung the guard to the floor and raised the pistol toward the armed guards.

A flurry of gunshots rang out through the corridor.

Zack lay motionless on the floor, staring up blankly. Everything faded to blackness. A trickle of blood spilled from the crooked grin on his face.

Free, at last.

Cavern of Hope

A COLD BREEZE LADEN with the damp smell of mold drifted out of the immense cavern opening. I stood, staring into the darkness ahead and dreading the task before me. Over the last week, my condition had grown steadily worse. My muscles had become so weak. I ached from head to toe. And, as of yesterday, my sight had begun to fail.

Knowing that standing there and dreading it wasn't getting me any closer to the exceptionally rare vyourin plant, I lit up a torch, took in a deep breath, and marched into the cavern.

Other than my sword, my only supplies were a water skin, some torches, a flint and steel, and a small pack of dried rations.

It was my hope to find the vyourin plant, which only grows in the lowest depths of caverns, and then make a quick exit before confronting any of the denizens that inhabit such places. If the sages were right, the vyourin plant would provide the cure I sought.

Cautious step by cautious step, I worked my way deeper into the cavern. The inspiring words received from the locals kept running through my mind.

"Better off goin back home and spending what time you have left with your loved ones."

"There are things in those caverns that will make you think dying is a good thing."

And the twist of the blade, "I don't think anyone in the last five years has found any vyourin in them caverns, at least those that made it back out haven't."

True words of encouragement, but I really didn't care. If I met my death in the depth of these caverns, that just meant I wouldn't have to wait for this cursed affliction to do it.

On I plodded. The light from my torch danced across the wet cavern walls, ushering my decent into the shadowy depths. The floor of the cavern was unusually smooth and sloped downward steeply. I kept one hand against the wall to steady myself. My trembling legs were already burning. Even if I found the vyourin, I had serious concerns about being able to make it back out. Unfortunately, I had no other options.

My foot caught on something solid, tripping me and sending me sprawling face down on the cold stone. The torch flew from my hand and rolled to a stop several feet on down the tunnel.

With a groan, I rolled over onto my back and stared up into the silence. How weak I had grown over the last few months. My left ankle still bore the mark of my affliction; an unhealed wound from the sting of a wulvrin scorpion. So odd that such a small and fragile creature had the power to forever change my life. "Life is strange like that", was what my uncle Grennen would often say.

The silence here was eerie, disturbed only by the sounds of my hoarse breathing and the low crackling of the burning torch. Then something moved in the distance, not far beyond where my torch lay.

I sat up as quickly, and quietly, as I could. It felt as if every hair on my body was standing on end. My mind raced wildly at the thought of what was moving in the darkness. I held my breath as I listened. There it was again, and it was definitely getting closer.

Slowly, I drew my sword from its leather sheath and peered into the darkness beyond my torch, straining to see the source of the noise.

There it was again. It sounded like something large sliding across the cavern floor. A shadowy form, low to the floor, took shape as it entered the light from my torch. I shifted to get a better look. With a hiss, the torch went out, plunging me into complete darkness.

Oh great! I got back onto my feet and began quietly backing up the corridor. I needed to put some distance between whatever was approaching and myself.

A low, guttural growl echoed through the tunnel, sending a chill up my spine. Oh please, just let it go away. In my present condition, there was no way I could put up much of a fight, not to mention I couldn't see a thing, which probably wasn't the case for whatever was coming for me.

I kneeled and laid my sword at my feet, wincing at the clink of metal on the stone cavern floor. I flipped open my leather pack and dug out another torch and placed it between my knees. With trembling hands, I slipped the flint and steel from my belt pouch and struck it over the head of the torch.

Each strike of the flint revealed a grotesque shape approaching. The thing was just a few feet away when the torch finally burst to life, illuminating the tunnel and fully revealing my pursuer.

It was a grotesque creature that looked very much like a giant turtle, but with exceptionally long, clawed arms in the front and a large tail covered with numerous, white spikes. The thing was at least four feet in length and looked to weigh several hundred pounds.

The creature pulled back from the light of the torch, squinting its huge eyes in obvious pain. Taking advantage of the opportunity, I scooped up my sword and rushed forward. I hoped to get past the creature before it could recover from the blinding effect of my torch.

Just as I moved past it, the creature lashed out with its tail, striking me between the shoulders. It was a solid and powerful hit, knocking me off my feet and sending me rolling down the tunnel. This time I managed to hold onto my torch. My sword, however, went sliding across the floor. A series of clangs echoed through the tunnel, each fainter than the last. Unless I was mistaken, I had just lost my only weapon, likely into a pit or over a ledge.

As quickly as I could manage, I got back on my feet, scrambling on down the tunnel. I paused briefly at the location where I last saw my sword sliding away and, as I feared, there was a wide crevice in the floor. It was deeper than my torchlight could penetrate, and there was no sign of my sword. There was nothing I could do about it, so on I ran.

Angry hisses and the scuffing sounds of pursuit echoed after me as I fled deeper into the cavern. The light from my torch revealed many small holes and side tunnels. How many other creatures were holed up in here, ready to make a meal of me? I fought down my terror and kept moving. I had to stay focused.

A warm trickle slid down my back causing my shirt to cling

to me with sticky wetness. I could only hope I wasn't losing too much blood.

Fortunately, the creature moved fairly slowly. Unfortunately, so did I, and from the sounds coming from behind, it was gaining on me.

Just ahead, the tunnel made a sharp turn to the right. The light from my torch revealed that the tunnel also narrowed significantly at that point. I ran on as fast as my feeble legs could carry me, hoping against hope that the turn in the tunnel would be too narrow for my pursuer to enter.

As I made the turn, I immediately saw that the tunnel narrowed to a small slit not wider than two feet. I was fairly certain the creature wouldn't be able to fit through it. I just hoped that I could.

Turning sideways, I slid into the narrow opening. But before I was able to get all the way in, an explosion of pain shot up my left leg. I turned to see the creature's long neck and head stuck into the crevice. Its curved beak was sunk deep into my left calf. Its neck retracted, pulling me violently to the ground and back out into the open.

I clawed against the stone floor, struggling to pull free. I managed to grab hold of a rocky protrusion with one hand. The creature pulled hard, doing its best to drag me further away from my route of escape. I held on for dear life. If I let go now, it would be the end.

I rolled onto my side and thrust my torch into the creature's face. There was a loud hiss, and a burst of smoke as the flames burned into the creature's moist skin. It let out a high-pitched screech, simultaneously releasing its grip on my leg.

I immediately pushed and backpedaled my way back into the narrow slit. The beast lunged forward, slamming hard into the opening. Its head and long neck lunged in for me but fell short. It snapped and screeched, desperately trying to get to me, but this time I was safely out of its reach.

Just a few feet further in, the tunnel widened, allowing more freedom of movement. I used the room to fall onto my back, completely exhausted.

After several minutes of vain struggling, the creature retreated back into the darkness.

It took several more minutes to catch my breath and convince myself I could continue.

With a painful moan, I forced myself to sit up. The creature's bite had left a gaping wound in my calf that was bleeding profusely. I tore a strip from my shirt and tied it around the wound.

My whole body throbbed with pain. I wondered if it would be better to just die now and be free from this agony, but I was far too stubborn to entertain such thoughts for long.

Gritting my teeth in pain, I got back onto my feet. Just a few feet further in, the tunnel abruptly widened back out to at least thirty feet across. Before leaving the safety of the narrow section, I held my breath, peering into this new section of tunnel and listening for anything moving or breathing. It was deathly quiet, but I could imagine another horrifying predator lying in wait for me just beyond the reach of my torch light.

I cautiously stepped out into the open, glancing in every direction. Clear so far. Not wanting to waste any more time, I limped on into the depths of the cavern.

Several hours, and three torches later, I stood at the mouth of a large, level section of cavern. I had already found, and searched, two other such areas, neither of which held anything resembling plant life, let alone the vyourin plant I sought. Still, I couldn't help but feel excited knowing that this could be the one. I could be mere feet away from the cure to my suffering and imminent death. Draining the last drop of water from my water skin, I anxiously limped forward.

Huge stalactites hung from the ceiling like the fangs of some enormous serpent. Several large boulders and jagged slabs of rock lay strewn about the floor, apparently from portions of the ceiling that had broken free. How many tons of unstable rock hung over my head? I tried not to think about it.

Scanning the floor for any sign of plant life, I slowly advanced. My torch was burning low and wasn't putting out a great deal of light, but with only two left, I had to make each one last as long as possible. I had already been in here longer

than I had hoped I would.

The ground here gave under foot. Unlike the other areas of this cavern, this area was more soil and loose dirt than rock. My hopes soared with renewed fervor.

A noise off to my left caused me to jump. My first impression was that a portion of the ceiling had fallen, but then I felt it. A strong vibration resonated beneath my feet. Probably just a small trimmer. I moved deeper into the cavern, picking my way around the boulders and rocks.

A warm tingle started at the bottom of my feet and steadily spread up into the rest of my body. With each step, the tingling grew stronger. Once the sensation reached my head, I immediately felt the presence of another being. It was as if someone were calling to me, though I heard no voice or words.

The feeling was unlike anything I had experienced before, and though I had no idea what was causing it, it didn't frighten me in the least. It actually calmed me. Suddenly, I didn't feel so alone.

I stepped around a slab of rock twice as tall as I was, and a flicker of gold reflected back at me from the cavern floor. My heart raced as I approached for a closer look. I nearly fell over with disbelief when I realized what I was seeing. It was the vyourin plant! Its glossy, golden leaves sparkled in the light of

my torch.

I dropped to my knees and stabbed the butt of my torch into the soft dirt of the floor and hastily began digging around the base of the plant with both hands. After exposing its roots, I carefully pulled it free from the soil, making sure that I left none of the roots behind.

Its roots were thick and round, and as black as the cavern in which it grew. I tossed a piece into my mouth, chewing it up as quickly as I could. The bitterness made my eyes squint, and the gritty crunch of dirt didn't add to its appeal. I savored it just the same.

I pulled up my torch and walked around the immediate area, hoping to find more of the rare plant. Nothing. It was likely that this was the only vyourin plant in the entire cavern. Hopefully, it was enough.

My torch flickered and popped as it ate at the last bit of cloth and pitch. I pulled out another torch and placed it in the dying flames. The cavern lit up brighter as the fresh torch burst to life. I tossed the expended torch to the side.

The moment the expended torch hit the ground, I felt the vibrations again, and then the floor exploded beneath it.

A gigantic, worm-like creature shot up out of the ground, swallowing the torch and a large portion of the ground around it. Bits of dirt and rock sprayed out in all directions before raining back down to the floor.

The creature's entire body was covered with curved spikes that resembled horns, each as long as my hand. It slammed back down into the floor headfirst. The impact sounded like thunder within the confines of the cavern. With a few powerful twists of its body, it disappeared from sight.

I stood motionless, in complete awe. I felt the strong vibrations in the ground for a few more seconds, and then all was calm once more. Afraid to move, and struggling to keep my legs from trembling, I stood motionless.

The feeling of something calling to me came again, much stronger and clearer this time. I gazed around the room in search of what the source of this strange sensation could be, and then I saw it.

Maybe thirty feet away, in the same area from which the worm had emerged, a sword lay in the loose dirt turned up by the worm. The sword's handle and hilt glowed a soft blue and the blade gleamed with the luster of polished silver. I had the distinct feeling the sword wanted me to come to it, but how could that be? Though it made no sense, I couldn't resist the urge. I knew I had to get that sword.

Moving as subtly as I could, I reached into the small sack tied to my side and pulled out a pack of rations. The wound in my leg throbbed with pain and I felt so drained. This likely wouldn't buy me much time, if any. I would have to move quickly. I just prayed I had the strength to.

I slung the pack of rations as far toward the back of the cavern as I could manage. The worm took the bait. The ground shook violently as a ripple of earth and rock parted the floor, making a straight line toward the rations.

I ran with all the strength I could manage, but as I feared, my injured leg betrayed me. It gave out with the first step, landing me flat on my face. With a loud curse, I pushed back to my feet and pushed on, hopping as much as running.

I glanced over my shoulder and saw the wave of earth turn and head toward me. I struggled forward with all I had. I had to reach that sword.

With the worm only a few feet behind me, and closing fast, I reached the sword. Various runes and golden symbols decorated the full length of the silver blade. The blade itself looked flawless. No scratches, dirt, or rust marred its mirror finish.

Without stopping, I snatched up the sword and kept on moving, making for the small tunnel that led out of the chamber. Rocks and dirt pelted me from behind. The worm had to be nearly on top of me.

With every step I took, strengthening jolts of energy, similar to what I felt when I first entered the worm's lair, raced through my body. It was coming from the sword!

My struggling steps became powerful strides as the pain and

weakness fled my body. With one final thrust, I leaped the final eight feet or so to the tapering end of the tunnel, doing a complete forward roll and sliding to a stop several feet from the loose dirt of the worm's lair.

A shower of dirt cascaded over me as the approaching wave of earth came to a halt where the loose dirt of the room met the hard, rock floor of the tunnel. Apparently, it couldn't pursue me into the tunnel. I surprised myself with my own outburst of laughter.

"Not today, worm," I said, feeling exhilarated by the energy flooding into my muscles.

Not wanting to press my luck, I sprang to my feet and sprinted up the tunnel, making for the exit.

I ran, without slowing, for several minutes. At last, I had to pause to catch my breath. I stared with a mix of confusion and awe at the marvelous sword in my hand. I had just been running, and with little to no pain. And my sight; I could see every wonderful detail of the tunnel around me. The way the tiny rivulets of water made their way down the smooth surface of the walls, the brilliant flickering flames of my torch and the dancing shadows they projected, and the intricate detail of the sword I now held.

This was clearly no ordinary sword. I had heard of such things, but never really believed they existed. A thought came to mind. What if I were to... A sickening wave of dizziness and weakness overwhelmed me as soon as I let go of the sword, dropping to my knees.

The injury in my leg bloomed with pain, and my whole body groaned in protest.

I quickly snatched up the sword. As before, the warm jolts of energy flowed up my arm and then throughout my entire body. The pain and weakness left almost instantly.

The sword couldn't have fit my hand more perfectly. It emanated a warmth and strength that was almost intoxicating. As crazy as it seemed, it felt as if the sword was happy to be held. I was certainly happy to be holding *it*. With the aid of this sword, I just might make it out of this wretched hole.

I sped back through the tunnels, basking in the renewed strength coursing through my body. I could still feel the wound in my leg, but it didn't hinder me. How strong would the sword make me once the vyourin ran its course and healed my affliction?

As I neared a fork in the tunnel, I suddenly realized that I shouldn't be coming to a fork. I turned about, studying the section of tunnel in which I stood. None of this looked familiar.

Blast it! I must have taken a wrong turn while daydreaming like a fool child. I had no choice but to turn back and look for a section of tunnel that was familiar.

For at least half an hour, I backtracked, looking carefully at every turn for something familiar that would tell me which way I needed to go. Growing increasingly concerned, and with exhaustion creeping in, I plopped down onto the floor and leaned back against the wall.

I wedged my torch into a crack in the floor and rested my head on my knees. I just needed to rest for a few minutes and regain my focus.

A deep growl brought my head up with a start. I pulled the torch free and leaped to my feet, sword in hand. I didn't have to wait long before a familiar creature with long, clawed arms and a barbed tail charged out of the darkness toward me. I gripped my sword with a white-knuckled fist and readied myself.

The creature didn't slow, charging straight for me with its beak snapping in hungry anticipation. Its long talons clicked against the stone floor with each step.

With a yell, I leaped forward, swinging the gold and silver blade in a sweeping blow aimed for the creature's head. The beast drew its head back with surprising speed. My blade sung past, narrowly missing.

The creature immediately retaliated, whipping its thick, spiked tail forward. I pulled my sword up to intercept, barely getting it up in time to keep the tail from smashing into my head. The strength of the blow was tremendous, nearly knocking the sword from my hand.

Again the creature attacked, this time lunging toward my legs. I leaped backward, barely avoiding the snapping maw. I squared my feet and brought my sword down hard, striking the creature on the top of the head. The silver blade bit in deep, opening a large gash in the beast's dark hide. It screeched in pain and shook its head, sending huge drops of blood spattering to the floor.

I struck again, this time leading with the sword's tip in hopes of skewing the beast, but before I could finish the thrust, it swept its tail out low, catching me around the ankles and knocking my feet out from under me.

The impact knocked the breath out of my lungs. The beast lashed out with an arm, driving several long talons through my sword hand, and sending my sword skidding across the floor. I kicked out with my uninjured leg, connecting squarely with the side of the creature's head. It seemed not to notice at all.

Before I had time to do anything more, all my strength melted away like wax in a smith's forge. All the plagues of my affliction, as well as the injuries.I had recently received, came crashing back upon me in a flood of pain and fatigue.

I tried to kick the creature away from me, but my weak blows did little to deter the bulky mass of the hungry predator. It pounced on top of my legs and stomach pinning me helplessly to the floor. For a brief second, it peered into my eyes, then lunged forward with its powerful neck, mouth open wide.

Its cold beak sunk deep into the tender flesh of my neck. My eyes felt as if they were coming out of their sockets. With a sickly crunch and one final quiver of my body, everything

went dark.

I jerked upright with a loud gasp and jumped to my feet, turning about in all directions with the sword held out in front of me. The torch was burning low on the floor, still wedged in the crack where I had placed it. My body was wet with sweat, and my heart was racing. I must have fallen asleep. It was just a dream!

I breathed a huge sigh of relief and rubbed my neck thankfully. I took the last torch from my pack and lit it from the one stuck in the floor before setting out once more. I had to find my way out of here and quickly. The thought of wandering these tunnels with no light put a knot in my stomach.

I had gone no more than a hundred yards from where I had taken my pleasant nap before a familiar rock formation came into view. I remembered this area well. There were three separate directions in which I could proceed. Now that I had my bearings, I had no trouble in choosing the correct one.

As I hurried through the winding tunnels and corridors, I felt a great relief. Every turn brought a familiar rock formation, ledge, or some other feature that assured me I was on the right path. If I remember correctly, I should be back to the cavern's exit very soon.

A few minutes later, I walked into a disturbingly familiar area. The tunnel tapered to a small slit about two feet wide. I moved right up to the narrow gap and stopped. After a long pause, I leaned in, peering into the tunnel beyond. It was empty.

Slowly, and cautiously, I slipped through the small opening, gripping my sword tightly. Once on the other side, I stood for a moment, looking and listening. Except for the pounding of my heart in my ears, all was quiet. I continued on much slower from here, trying not to make a sound.

As I rounded the next sharp turn in the tunnel, my hopes of quietly slipping out were shattered.

The turtle-looking creature that nearly had me for lunch in this same area lay smack in the center of the tunnel, facing my direction. Its long neck slowly extended as it rose up onto its clawed feet. If this thing were able to smile, I'm sure it would have been just then. The blasted thing had no doubt been laying there in wait for me since our first encounter.

"It will be different this time, old boy," I said, waving my new sword in front of me.

The creature let out a deep growl as it started toward me, sweeping its barbed tail from side to side. I dropped the torch on the ground and poised myself for the fight.

As soon as it was within range, I lunged forward, driving the sword's tip toward the creature's neck. It recoiled with incredible speed, but not quite fast enough. The tip of the sword penetrated the beast's neck, but only slightly. The runes on the blade flashed with blue light for just an instant. I immediately followed with a downward slash, connecting on the creature's shoulder. This time the sword bit deep and all the runes along the blade's length lit up with an intense blue glow. Blue and white sparks, like tiny lightning bolts, leaped from the blade, striking the creature in a dozen places. Everywhere they made contact, the flesh turned white and blistered.

The creature hissed in pain and lashed out with its tail. I leaped backwards, but the tip of its spiked tail still managed to hit me, tearing open the front of my shirt and drawing several deep lines of blood across my stomach.

Blood poured in steady rivulets from the creature's wound. Its right arm was ruined, and it was clearly off balance. As it lurched forward for another attack, I dropped to one knee and swung my sword in a low, wide arc. The flawless blade sliced through the beast's other arm, completely severing it. As before, the sparks of energy showered forth, burning into the creature's flesh.

The creature bellowed an ear-piercing cry, thrashing wildly and rolling on the floor. Putrid-smelling blood gushed from the severed stump.

I backed up several paces, getting well clear of the monster. It thrashed for several more seconds, then its movements began to slow. Finally, it went still, amidst a growing puddle of its own blood.

I inched toward it, holding my torch over its body and straining to see any signs of life left in the thing. I gave it a jab with the tip of my sword and jumped back. It didn't move.

Satisfied that it was dead, I stepped around it and backed on up the tunnel several feet before turning and running for the exit, the rush of adrenaline spurring me on.

Finally, the sunlit opening to the surface peeked out from above the next slope. I actually made it!

I stood in front of the cavern exit, smiling and breathing in the sweet, fresh air. Taking one last look at the dark entrance of the cavern, I turned and started the long descent down the mountain.

It was crazy to think that the deliverance from my creature-induced affliction came from deep within the bowels of a creature-infested cavern.

Life is strange like that.

A Wolf's Cry

JAME LOPED ACROSS THE WIDE PRAIRIE, energized by the crisp morning air. The sun had just broken over the horizon, casting a warm glow across the land. Jame felt so alive, so free. He ran faster, feeling the wind rush over his fur.

Despite its dry, rugged appearance this was a beautiful place. Bright purple flowers decorated many of the emerald shrubs and plants dotting the countryside. The sweet scents of spring lingered in the air.

A rabbit darted from a bush, zigzagging away and kicking up a trail of dust. Jame turned and gave chase, running the rabbit into a dense patch of cactuses. He sniffed and poked his nose into the prickly sanctuary before deciding it wasn't worth the effort.

Jame's chest swelled and collapsed like a giant bellows as he panted. His long tongue hung out to one side, bobbing with each breath. A sense of emptiness, or maybe more a feeling that something was just wrong, crept into his awareness. He tried to focus on the source of his concern but found it hard to concentrate.

Somewhere in the distance, another wolf let out a long, mournful cry. Jame's ears snapped to attention. He stood tall, frozen. His attention fully captured by the sound. The wolf's cry touched him to the depths of his soul. The emptiness he had felt suddenly swelled within him. It tugged at him, urging him to move. He had to find this wolf.

Jame sprinted off, ascending a steep slope with just a few powerful leaps. Several towering rock formations leaned at precarious angles, stretching into the sky. He paused to scan the area ahead, nose raised high, sniffing the air for any sign of the wolf.

A red hawk soared on outstretched wings high above the rocks. The world started spinning. The rocks and sky blurred and twisted together. Jame's vision faded to black before snapping back into focus.

Jame stood in front of a tall, clear window, staring out at the massive expanse of pavement and its dozens of intersecting roads. An enormous plane slowly glided down out of the sky touching down with a loud, but brief screech.

In the distance, another plane was just pulling away from the earth, its nose lifting into the sky as it started its climb. Dozens of people milled about in a rush; pulling large suitcases on wheels, talking on cell phones, standing in long lines.

In a blink, everything changed. Jame looked around at the sunbaked landscape all around him. He had no idea where he was. He knew that he was on his way somewhere, and he was certain it was important, but he just couldn't remember. He was so thirsty.

Jame slowly trotted around the side of the hill, making his way toward a shallow stream. He had the unshakable feeling that something was very out of place. He tried to put it out of his mind. It was a beautiful day, and he planned to enjoy it. Perhaps he would find a shady spot beneath one of the cliff's overhangs and stretch out for a while.

Jame stepped up to the edge of the stream, now nearly dried up. A thin trickle of water gathered into a shallow pool. He eagerly lapped at the water. It wasn't very cold, but it would do. He jumped backed, startled at a sudden movement near the pool's edge.

A fish lay on the rocks just short of the water's edge. It flopped feebly, mouth opening and closing in silent gasps. Its eyes were glazed over with a white film, dried out from the relentless sun. Such a terrible and slow death, he thought.

The ground fell away from Jame's feet, spinning and mixing in a dizzying blur.

Jame sat on a stool beside a low bed with a tall, oak headboard. He held the hand of a woman with long, black hair. Her cheekbones stood out beneath her gaunt skin. Dark bags hung below her tired, brown eyes. He knew he hadn't shown it as he should, but Jame loved her deeply. His heart ached for her. She was suffering terribly, and there was nothing he could do to help her.

He leaned over and gently kissed her on the forehead. Her lips spread the narrowest bit as she forced a smile. He tenderly tucked her blanket up under her chin before standing.

Jame turned to the woman waiting in the doorway, holding a tray with a bowl of soup. "Take good care of her," he said. "I'll be back in a few days."

He started out of the room but stopped in the doorway. He turned back to the woman on the bed. She stared at him but said nothing. There was so much pain in her eyes.

The howl of a distant wolf grabbed Jame's attention. He was still standing beside the small pool of water. The fish now lay motionless on the dry ground near the fleeting water's edge. A rising panic crept over him. Where was he? What was happening to him?

Another long cry from a wolf echoed from somewhere beyond the ridge. Jame's hackles stood up. A sense of longing washed over him. He knew something was terribly wrong. He felt that he should know what it was, but it escaped him. Tantalizing hints of understanding hung just out of his reach. He could sense them, but couldn't quite grasp them. He had to find this other wolf. Of that much, he was certain.

Jame continued up a gently sloping hill, determined to find answers. A dense wall of weeds and brambles covered the hillside near its crest. Not willing to waste time with finding a way around, Jame lowered his head and plowed in.

Briars and weeds grabbed at his head and legs and pulled at his fur as he pushed on. More than once, he found himself completely entangled and had to wriggle and thrash to work free, leaving patches of his grey fur behind in the process. His legs stung from numerous cuts and scratches, but he paid it little attention.

Jame finally emerged from the dense thicket, his fur disheveled and riddled with bits of weeds and burrs as well as several patches of fresh blood. He sprinted the last few feet up to the top of the hill before finally stopping.

He took a minute to catch his breath, admiring the beauty around him. The wind picked up, bending the tall green weeds below. The scent of cactus blooms danced around him, and then something else—the faint scent of smoke. The landscape lurched and twisted, rushing away in a blur.

Jame was seated, cross-legged, on the ground beside a small fire contained inside a circle of stones. On the opposite side of the fire sat a man with long, white hair. Deep creases, like cracks in sunbaked mud, ran over every inch of his dark skin. Heavy smears of white, black, and red paint decorated his cheeks. A turquoise band, adorned with several teeth that looked like they could be from a wolf, was tied around his head. Similar bands stood out around both of his upper arms as well.

The man sat motionless, staring into the flames. After a long pause, he tossed a branch full of red leaves into the fire. The fire snapped and raged, sending thick white smoke roiling into the air. The man looked up at Jame, and sorrow filled his aged, brown eyes.

"Sonya came back to us—to her home. She knew her time was short." He leaned forward, his eyes taking on a hard edge. "She was so lonely," he said.

Sonya. The name echoed through his mind. Jame's breath caught. An avalanche of memories crashed into him, memories of his life, not as a wolf, but as a man; a successful businessman. The relentless business meetings, traveling, planning, time away from home. He remembered it all now.

A chill danced across his skin as more memories surfaced. His wife, Sonya, was dead. She had been such a fighter. He had been so sure she was going to beat it, but the rare blood disease proved to be the stronger. She had died with her family, at the reservation, while he was away on an extended business trip in Japan. The guilt twisted his gut.

Jame forced himself to look the old man in the eyes. He now remembered Eowa, Sonya's father, quite well. Eowa had never approved of their marriage. *How he must resent me.*

The smoke from the fire grew thicker, settling around them both. It burned his lungs and stung his eyes. Jame squeezed his eyes shut, coughing as tears ran down both cheeks.

The ground seemed to tilt under him for just an instant before going still once more. Jame reluctantly opened his eyes. He was standing on top of a hill. He spun about looking for Eowa. He was alone.

Jame arched his neck over his back, nipping at a sudden itch before settling down on his haunches. He fought to make sense of all that was happening, trying to let it all sink in.

Sonya often spoke of her father, of how he held to the ancient ways of her people. More specifically, communing with spirits. Jame had never thought of it as more than naïve superstition. Clearly, he was wrong. Eowa had done this to him. Was this repayment for not being there for Sonya? Had he become the target of Eowa's pain and grief?

The breeze shifted and Jame caught the lingering scent of smoke. Maybe Eowa was still at the camp. He leaped down the hill, soaring over the high grass and landing on loose rock. He slid for several feet then broke into a run.

Jame ran as fast as he could, weaving past ragged shrubs and cactuses, many now brown from their extended lack of water. What if Eowa refused to change him back? A simmering rage rose within him. He had done everything in his power to provide for Sonya and give her the best life possible. "Everything except be there for her when she needed you most," the voice in his head whispered.

Jame shoved back the guilt. Eowa would undo this, or else. He was taken by surprise when something slammed into his side, knocking him to the ground. He slid to a stop and sprang back to his feet.

A large, snarling wolf approached him. Its fur was dark gray with black on the back of its ears and down each side of its neck. The wolf lowered its stance, and its ears lay back against the sides of its head. It continued to bear its teeth as it stalked forward.

Jame thought for a moment that this could be the wolf he had been searching for, but he felt no draw to this one, only aggression. No, this was the alpha male of the area.

He doubted that he would be able to outrun this wolf, and judging by its sheer size, it wasn't likely that he would fare well

in a fight. Maybe he could bluff his way out of this confrontation.

Jame flattened his ears back and took a step toward the other wolf, letting out a deep warning growl.

The wolf responded by lunging at him.

Jame tried to jump out of the away but wasn't quick enough. The wolf crashed into him once again, latching onto the side of his neck with powerful jaws and pinning him to the ground.

He fought to get out from under the crazed wolf, but it had a firm grip on him. Its teeth bit in deeper as it shook its head wildly. Jame yelped in pain. This beast was going to kill him!

Using the sloping hillside to his advantage, Jame managed to roll to the side. He kicked out with his hind legs, breaking the wolf's hold and launching it several feet down the hill. The alpha wolf landed hard, sliding several feet and sending a spray of rock and dirt down the hill. It wasted no time in regaining its footing. Jame used the opportunity to do the same.

The wolf charged back up the hill, but Jame now had the advantage of higher ground. Jame sprang forward, mouth open wide, and managed to bite the other wolf in the face. One of his teeth sunk deep into its left eye. Jame felt it pop and immediately tasted the warm spray of fluid on his tongue.

The alpha wolf howled in pain and retreated several steps. It shook its head from side to side, sending large drops of blood spattering to the ground. Its eye was ruined.

Jame immediately launched another attack, angling in from his opponent's blinded side. The strategy worked. Jame latched onto the wolf's neck, biting down with all his strength and shaking hard as he pushed forward. They both tumbled and rolled down the hill, finally coming to an abrupt stop against a large boulder.

Jame managed to hold on, knowing that it was kill or be killed.

The wolf cried out, trying its best to roll away from him. It pulled its tail up between its legs and made no further attempts to fight back.

Jame let go but remained standing over the wolf. He bared his teeth and growled a warning.

Cautiously, the wolf slinked away, tail still tucked tightly between its legs.

Jame could smell the blood on his muzzle. He could also smell his own blood that now wet the fur on the side of his neck. Despite the stinging wound in his neck and the throbbing pain in his left shoulder, Jame stood tall, watching the wolf's retreat. Once it was out of sight, he scanned the valley and spotted a faint wisp of smoke in the distance.

He set out once more, hopeful that he would find Eowa at the camp. But how would he communicate with him? Jame tried to play it out in his mind but found it increasingly difficult to think in human terms.

It seemed like ages ago that he had sat down by the campfire with Sonya's father. How long had it actually been? Hours? Days? Weeks? He struggled to hold on to his human memories.

* * *

Exhausted and bleeding, Jame limped into the camp. Half a dozen wooden poles with the likeness of wolves, rabbits, and other wild creatures carved into their surface formed a circle around the section of bare ground. In between the decorated poles stood stacks of flat rocks, painted with patterns of black, gray, and red. An assortment of flowers, berries, nuts, and herbs was laid out atop each of them.

In the center of the camp sat Eowa, cross-legged in front of the smoldering remnants of a campfire, arms folded expectantly.

"Why have you done this to me?" Jame asked, or at least meant to. The only sound that came forth was an odd-sounding growl.

"I have given you a very special opportunity, Jame," Eowa said, his expression unreadable.

Jame was not amused. He growled, in earnest this time, and stalked forward. Then he noticed the form lying on the ground behind Eowa. He froze.

A wool blanket woven with a host of red, black, and white triangular patterns was spread out over the body, covering all but the face—Jame's face.

He stared in numb silence. He knew it was his body lying there, but it felt as though he was looking at a stranger.

A sound from behind caught Jame's attention; his senses seemed so acute now. He turned to see a lanky, female wolf standing only a few feet away. Her fur was as dark as midnight. She tilted her head to the side as she studied him. Her deep yellow eyes seemed to peer into his soul.

The recognition was immediate, the emotions overwhelming. Jame's spirit soared. The gnawing void within him vanished, replaced with indescribable joy and relief.

He didn't know how it was that he knew, but there was no doubt. He knew this wolf. It was Sonya. He rushed to her, tail wagging excitedly, and began licking her face. They nuzzled and licked each other for several moments before finally separating.

Eowa stood with a groan. "She held on for as long as she could." Eowa smiled at Sonya affectionately. "I gave her spirit a new home before it could flee from her dying body."

This all seemed so ludicrous, yet here he was, a wolf, staring at his wife that he thought was dead, but who was now, apparently, also a wolf. In spite of the circumstances, Jame was warmed with a feeling of contentment that he hadn't known in many years.

"You have a choice, Jame. Stay here with Sonya, as you are, or return to your body. You must decide quickly. Your human body will not last much longer unless I return your spirit."

Both Eowa and Sonya stared at him in silence. Jame looked to each of them, and then to his body lying on the ground.

"The decision is permanent. I will not be able to do this for you again," Eowa said. "Remain by Sonya if you wish to remain as you are. Lie next to your body if you do not."

A million thoughts collided and fought within his mind. Finally, he lowered his head and slowly walked over to his body. He carefully took the blanket in his teeth and pulled it up over the face of the body that used to belong to him.

Jame turned back toward Sonya and then loped to her side. They jumped about one another, barking with excitement.

When they finally calmed, they stood side by side, facing Eowa. Tears ran down his aged face. He smiled wide and nodded in approval.

Jame and Sonya approached him.

Eowa knelt and put an arm around each of their necks, hugging them tightly. "I love you, daughter," he said, placing his forehead against Sonya's. Sonya licked his face.

"Take care of her," he said, giving Jame a serious look.

Jame nodded his head.

"Go on you two," Eowa said, gesturing toward the open prairie.

Side by side, with the love of his life, Jame walked away.

He never looked back.

www.ingramcontent.com/pod-product-compliance
Lightning Source LLC
Chambersburg PA
CBHW021549310726

48972CB00003B/747